The Moment He Touched Kristin
He Knew It Was A Mistake.

She looked at him and he felt as if he'd been
hit in the stomach. Breathless. Gasping for air.
Her eyes were as green as emeralds sparkling in
sunshine. Soft and vulnerable. A bolt of attraction
shot through him with the unexpected ferocity of
a clap of summer thunder.

All these years they'd been friends and he'd never
been more aware of her physically. Her hands were
warm, her skin was silky and he resisted the urge to
smooth his thumb across the tender flesh. Cut it out,
Derek, he chided himself.

He'd begun to think of her as a woman rather than
the girl he'd felt responsible for all these years.

What was he going to do about Kristin?

Dear Reader,

Welcome to Silhouette Desire and another month of sensual tales. Our compelling continuity DYNASTIES: THE DANFORTHS continues with the story of a lovely Danforth daughter whose well-being is threatened and the hot U.S. Navy SEAL assigned to protect her. Maureen Child's *Man Beneath the Uniform* gives new meaning to the term *sleepover!*

Other series this month include TEXAS CATTLEMAN'S CLUB: THE STOLEN BABY with Cindy Gerard's fabulous *Breathless for the Bachelor.* Seems this member of the Lone Star state's most exclusive club has it bad for his best friend's sister. Lucky lady! And Rochelle Alers launches a brand-new series, THE BLACKSTONES OF VIRGINIA, with *The Long Hot Summer,* which is set amid the fascinating world of horse-breeding.

Anne Marie Winston singes the pages with her steamy almost-marriage-of-convenience story, *The Marriage Ultimatum.* And in *Cherokee Stranger* by Sheri WhiteFeather, a man gets a second chance with a woman who wants him for her first time. Finally, welcome brand-new author Michelle Celmer with *Playing by the Baby Rules,* the story of a woman desperate for a baby and the hunky man who steps up to give her exactly what she wants.

Here's hoping Silhouette Desire delivers exactly what *you* desire in a powerful, passionate and provocative read!

Best,

Melissa Jeglinski

Melissa Jeglinski
Senior Editor, Silhouette Desire

Please address questions and book requests to:
Silhouette Reader Service
U.S.: 3010 Walden Ave., P.O. Box 1325, Buffalo, NY 14269
Canadian: P.O. Box 609, Fort Erie, Ont. L2A 5X3

The
MARRIAGE
ULTIMATUM

ANNE MARIE WINSTON

Published by Silhouette Books
America's Publisher of Contemporary Romance

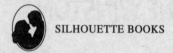 **SILHOUETTE BOOKS**

ISBN 0-373-76562-2

THE MARRIAGE ULTIMATUM

Copyright © 2004 by Anne Marie Rodgers

This edition published by arrangement with Harlequin Books S.A.

Visit Silhouette at www.eHarlequin.com

Printed in U.S.A.

Books by Anne Marie Winston

ANNE MARIE WINSTON

RITA® Award finalist and bestselling author Anne Marie Winston loves babies she can give back when they cry, animals in all shapes and sizes and just about anything that blooms. When she's not writing, she's managing a house full of animals and teenagers, reading anything she can find and trying *not* to eat chocolate. She will dance at the slightest provocation and weeds her gardens when she can't see the sun for the weeds anymore. You can learn more about Anne Marie's novels by visiting her Web site at www.annemariewinston.com.

In memory of Winston's Shining Fancy, C.D., C.G.C.
1990–2002
From the shelter straight into my heart
Forever my sweet boy

One

"**D**erek, I think we should get married."

"You think we—*what?*" Derek Mahoney almost dropped the instrument he was using to place sutures in a setter's paw. Sensing a break in the veterinarian's concentration, the animal tried to flounder to its feet.

Kristin Gordon shifted her grip on the squirming canine she was holding for Derek. Her thick, curly braid slid forward and she flipped it back out of the way with an impatient toss of her head. "I said I think we should get married."

"Oh." Derek grinned and relaxed. Kristin hadn't changed a bit since she was a teenager. She still came up with all kinds of wild ideas. "Sure thing, Kris. Do you think we could fit it in during my lunch break?"

Kristin's green eyes narrowed as she studied him over the top of the dog's head. Her dark brows, striking against her porcelain skin, rose and drew together in what Derek recognized as a temper-pending, "This-is-not-a-joke" look. "Derek, I'm—"

"Serious," he said in unison with her.

"Morning, Dr. Mahoney. Hi, Kristin. Thanks for filling in for me. When I dropped my kids off at school, I realized I had a flat tire." Faye, Derek's veterinary technician, breezed into the Quartz Forge Animal Clinic, still buttoning her lab coat. "How's old Princess doing?"

"She looks great for a twelve-year-old dog that tangled with a mower blade." Derek lifted the animal and set her gently on the floor, grateful for the change of subject. "Mrs. Peters is in the waiting room. You can take Princess out to her. No vigorous exercise, antibiotics, an Elizabethan collar if she chews at the stitches."

"Okay." Faye handed him a chart. "Mutley is coming in for exploratory surgery tomorrow. The owner would like to talk to you again before he goes under the knife."

Derek took the chart as he opened the door for Faye and the aging red setter to precede him.

"Derek?"

Reluctantly, he looked over his shoulder. For a minute there, he'd actually thought he was going to get out of the room without further discussion. "Kris." He inclined his head toward the door. "I have a waiting room full of anxious pet owners out there to see. You have to take care of my daughter and get back to your own work. Why don't we discuss the wedding plans tonight?''

"You're not taking this seriously." She was still frowning as she marched past him.

"You're right." He couldn't resist tugging on the end of her long, blond braid. He'd often teased her this way over the past ten years—since the first time he'd seen her when he'd come to the Pennsylvania mountains to interview with her father for the veterinary practice partnership Paul Gordon was advertising. She'd been a tomboyish sixteen-year-old then. These days, she wore her hair up in a practical, if often untidy style most of the time.

Other than that, she hadn't changed all that much, he thought in amusement as he surveyed her tall, slender figure clad in one of her father's old flannel shirts and a loose pair of khaki trousers. If it weren't for that glorious mane of curls, she could have been a boy.

"My daddy!"

Derek jerked up his head at the sound of the childish voice. He barely had time to catch his not-quite-three-year-old daughter as Mollie hurled herself down the hallway and into his arms.

"Hey, squirt." He rubbed his nose gently against hers. "Have you had fun playing with Sandy while Kristin helped me?" Sandy, his receptionist, wasn't confident handling big dogs. She'd volunteered to watch Mollie if Kristin would help Derek until Faye arrived.

"We made paper dolls!" Mollie waved the string of paper figures at him while she paused, clearly thinking of her next words. He drank in the sight of her big, earnest blue eyes, the rosy cheeks and fly-away dark curls.

What would he have done without her? Losing Deb had been the worst nightmare a man could ever have. One day, they'd been eagerly anticipating the birth of their first child. The next, he'd been hearing phrases like, "No options," "metastasize" and "can't risk radiation during the pregnancy." They'd spent the remaining nine weeks of Deb's pregnancy in a daze. It wasn't until two months after Mollie's birth, when he'd stood beside his wife's grave holding his healthy infant daughter in his arms, that he'd begun to realize the finality of what the doctors had told him.

Mollie was still chattering away as Kristin approached, holding the light jacket he'd put on his daughter this morning before he'd dropped her off at Kristin's town house. "Come on, Mols. Let's get your coat on and go play outside."

Derek set Mollie on the floor and she immediately ran to Kristin, who gave her a hug before stuffing her small arms into the coat. "Were you a good girl for Miss Sandy?"

"Yes." Mollie nodded positively.

"Great! I'm proud of you. Tell Daddy we'll see him at supper time."

"Bye, Daddy. See you at supper time," Mollie parroted, and he waved as Kristin led her out the back door. As the door closed behind them, he shook his head fondly. What a pair. The two were as close as sisters. He couldn't have asked for a better friend than Kristin over the past few years.

"Kristin takes mighty good care of that little girl of yours." Faye came back down the hallway carrying a cat that was scheduled for blood work.

Derek nodded. "I don't know what I'd do without her." Then he grinned, remembering how Kristin had shaken him up in the exam room. "But she sure does come up with some mighty strange schemes."

Faye smiled. She'd worked for Kristin's father, "Doc" Gordon, before Derek took over the practice and she'd known Kristin since she had been a young child. "Let me guess. She wants to start flying lessons."

"Nope."

"Join the police academy?"

Derek chuckled and shook his head.

"Take an Alaskan wilderness trek?"

"Not even close. She thinks I should marry her."

To his surprise, Faye didn't give an immediate belly laugh as he'd expected. "Hmm," was all she said. The matter-of-fact way she'd accepted the statement shook him more than he liked.

"What does 'hmm' mean?"

Faye shrugged. "It's a pretty good idea, if you ask me."

"Are you kidding?" He stopped dead. "She's way too young for me."

"You're thirty-four years old." Faye was over

fifty and she only shook her head. "That's young. And Kristin was twenty-five last week. You're not even a decade apart."

He stared at her, feeling ridiculously betrayed. He'd been sure Faye would laugh and agree with him about Kristin's harebrained idea. "It's a nutty idea, just like most of her other schemes."

She ignored his warning tone. "Mollie needs a mother. Who better than the woman who's cared for her since she was born? And you need a wife, but just anybody won't do. You need somebody who's as bullheaded as you, somebody who will bark back when you get difficult—"

"Kristin is hardly a woman." He knew his face mirrored the irritation he was feeling.

Faye hooted. "Give me a break, Derek. She ain't a man and she's way too old to be a teenager!"

"That may be, but she's not marriage material." His tone was curt as he turned away and continued down the hall before she could see the red flush he was pretty sure was climbing his face. Faye must be crazy. He had no intention of ever marrying again. Why should he? His life was just fine the way it was—as fine as it ever could be without Deb. No one could replace her in his heart.

Besides, Deb hadn't been bullheaded and they'd never had a shouting match in the entire ten years of their marriage. She was nothing like Kristin, a whirl-wind of opinionated energy. No, no one could ever be the same as his sweet, gentle Deb.

She'd been warm and loving, filling the world

around her with her own special brand of quiet peace until the cancer had extinguished her life and destroyed his. If it hadn't been for Mollie, their precious gift, thankfully untouched by the illness that ravaged her mother, he'd have laid down and died with Deb.

The thought of his bouncy baby girl soothed the deep sorrow that still filled him at the thought of living a lifetime without Deb. He was darn lucky to have such a handy arrangement with Kris. Mollie couldn't be in better hands.

Hands. Recalling the chart he still held, he remembered it was Friday and he had patients waiting. He wanted to be finished by noon so he could spend the afternoon doing well-checks on new arrivals at the Appalachian Animal Sanctuary, a nonprofit shelter Kristin's father had founded a few years before his death. Forcing himself to dismiss thoughts of Kristin, he went on down the hall to talk about Mutley.

But that evening, as he said farewell to the volunteers at the animal sanctuary's on-site clinic, Kristin's words were still replaying themselves in his ears. He hadn't been able to think of anything else today. Every time he'd surfaced from whatever procedure he was concentrating on, he heard her again. *I think we should get married.*

Crazy! He felt a sensation oddly akin to panic clutch at his chest as he parked in his driveway and walked up the front walk of his home. It was a beautiful old brick manor house in the small town of Quartz Forge, just minutes from the Michaux Forest and the Appalachian Trail. Kristin had shared it with her father until his sudden death from a heart attack nearly eight years ago. Just like Mollie, her own mother had passed away when she was an infant. After Paul Gordon had died, Kristin had claimed the place was too big for just her, so he'd bought it from her at generous fair-market value for the family he and Deb anticipated would fill it one day. Kristin had protested the amount, but he'd been firm. It wasn't as if he'd ever miss that amount of money, although Kristin didn't know that. No one in Quartz Forge knew the extent of his personal fortune and he was happy to keep it that way.

His personal fortune. The realization that he was a wealthy man—no, make that a filthy-rich man—still didn't seem real. Thanks to his brother's savvy dealings, the ten million he'd started with had increased significantly just in the fifteen years he'd had it. Maybe, he thought, he just didn't *want* it to be real. Because if it hadn't happened, his parents would still be alive and enjoying their first and only grandchild.

He still could barely think of them. In one of the most improbable scenarios ever, his parents had been swimming while on a second honeymoon in the Caribbean when they had been struck by a young drunk speedboat driver while Derek and his brother Damon were in high school. It turned out their killer was a Saudi prince. The young man's father, furious at his son's reckless behavior, settled a multimillion-dollar sum on the two Mahoney brothers and nullified the prince's position as his heir, elevating another of his sons instead. While it hadn't brought back his parents and it wasn't justice as Americans knew it, Derek imagined the punishment was far more effective in the long run than the suspended jail sentence the young man had received.

The heavy inner door opened while he was mounting the steps, interrupting his morose thoughts. Mollie appeared behind the screen, waving wildly. A moment later, Kristin appeared behind her. She glanced at him, unsmiling, and then stepped back, eyes averted, as he opened the door and walked inside.

"My daddy! My daddy!" Mollie chattered happily about her day as he swung her up into his arms for a hug. An instant later she was squirming to be set down, babbling something about Play-Doh that she apparently wanted him to see. As she raced out of the front hallway, he risked a glance at Kristin.

"Looks like you two had a fun afternoon. How long did she nap today?"

"Two hours." Kristin's voice was so carefully neutral that he could tell without a doubt she was still angry. She was normally the most expressive person he knew, her green eyes telegraphing joy or amusement or outrage or whatever it was she was feeling. "She woke up about four."

He checked the hallway. Mollie still hadn't reappeared. "Um, Kris, about what you said this morning?"

She didn't speak, only tilted her head and lifted her eyebrows in cool query.

"It's just not that easy." She was studying a spot just beyond his left shoulder and he had a shockingly strong impulse to grab her and shake her until she looked at him. "People don't just get married because it's convenient, or—or because it would solve a few logistical problems. You're a great baby-sitter and you know I'll never be able to thank you enough for the way you've stepped in to help me raise Mollie, but—" he made a helpless gesture "—that's no reason to try to force us into becoming a family."

There was a long silence in the hallway and he could hear his own awkward words echoing around them. Finally, when she still didn't respond, he demanded, "Do you understand what I'm trying to say?"

"Perfectly." Her voice was chilly. "You want to monopolize my life and my youth because it's a convenient arrangement for you."

He was shocked. "That's not true!" Was it?

"Look, Derek." Kristin's face took on the mutinous expression he knew from experience meant that he was going to have to use every trick in the book to change her opinion. Her tone went from cool to heated. "This isn't fair to me or to Molly. She's growing far too dependent on me. You're setting yourself up for trouble when you do get married again some day. She'll have a terrible time acclimating to a new mother."

"Dependent how?" The tone in her voice made him uneasy and he ignored the rest of her words because he had no idea how to respond. Why did he have to get married again? He was perfectly happy the way he was.

Or at least he had been. He wasn't sure where this was going but he was fairly sure he wasn't going to like where it ended.

"She's been calling me Mommy. Not often, but sometimes it just slips out. Given the amount of time we're together, it's probably natural—and that's what I wanted to talk about." She took a deep breath and her voice quavered. "I think you should find a new baby-sitter for Mollie."

He was stunned. No, not stunned. Sledgehammer-in-the-forehead totally shocked. He couldn't even formulate an answer. At that moment, Mollie came racing toward him again, demanding he see her art-work.

"There's a roast in the oven," Kristin said, "with carrots and potatoes. Mollie's had plenty of fruit and vegetables today so she could have some ice cream for dessert."

"You're not staying?" Kristin nearly always ate with them on weekday evenings.

"No." She turned away and took her jacket from the knob of the hall closet. "I've got some things to do this evening."

Darn Derek anyway!

The following afternoon, Kristin scowled at the columns of figures before her, but she couldn't concentrate on the quarterly taxes she should be completing for a local artist. Derek still thought of her as a giddy teenager, she could tell. Why couldn't he see how much she had changed and matured? He trusted her to raise his daughter, but he couldn't believe she was grown-up.

Well, that was going to change. She was tired of being good old helpful Kristin, part of the woodwork. Deb had died more than two years ago.

Sadness hovered, threatening to spirit away her righteous annoyance. She'd loved Deb like a sister. And had Deb lived, Kristin would never have acknowledged her own feelings for Derek as anything more than an adolescent crush. But she wasn't a teenager anymore. She was a woman. A woman who loved him deeply.

And he'd made it very clear today that he wasn't the least bit interested in changing the way he viewed her.

She sighed. Was it so wrong of her to want a family of her own and a love for the rest of her life? She was a good mother to Mollie and she knew the little girl loved her. But that wasn't enough.

She squeezed her eyes tightly shut, stubbornly denying tears. She was too practical to spend the rest of her life wishing for the moon. She was twenty-five years old, and she'd barely even given other men a second glance. All her life, she'd never been seriously attracted to anyone else…because she compared them all to Derek? There had been guys in college who had asked her out, but she hadn't been interested in developing any relationships. She'd had one sexual encounter so tepid it barely ranked as such.

And it was all Derek's fault. He still had been married then and she'd never even entertained the thought that he might be hers someday. Even so, he'd been the standard by which she'd judged other men, even if she hadn't realized it at the time.

But then Deb had died. And gradually, she'd acknowledged that her girlish love hadn't faded, hadn't died. It had simply matured into a woman's love. Her heart ached to heal him, but he wouldn't let her get close.

And Kristin wasn't going to spend the rest of her life waiting for Derek to wake up. If he didn't want her, it was time to move on. Her heart uttered a protest but she shushed it ruthlessly. Maybe there wasn't another Derek Mahoney out there, but there were plenty of men, good men who could love her, men with whom she could make a home and a family.

And if a corner of her heart would always belong to Derek, she would be the only one to know or care.

Decision made, she nodded to herself, then picked up her pencil, determined to accomplish something in the limited time she had. Mollie still napped during the day and Kristin found the quiet afternoons were one of her most productive times. The accounting work she did was portable and she simply brought it along with her when she came to Derek's house each afternoon.

It was a good arrangement. He dropped Mollie off in the morning. Kristin fed her breakfast. At noon, they went back to Derek's house for lunch and then Mollie napped while Kristin worked.

The only time it got a little hairy was during the

last frantic weeks of tax season, when she could work every hour of every day if she chose, and sometimes took on more than she should. But the money was good...and heaven knew she hadn't been in a position to turn down extra income over the years since her father had died. Not after the debts she'd discovered he'd left.

Actually, if she went to work full-time as an accountant, she would be able to pay off the remainder of the debt in a year or so, rather than the longer term she'd projected. That wouldn't be so bad, she encouraged herself.

Yes, it *had* been a good arrangement that she and Derek had had. But it was going to have to end.

Mollie woke shortly after four. Her schedule was fairly predictable unless she was ill, and Kristin let her help make a meat loaf for the evening meal. She had just taken the dish out of the oven at five-thirty when the front door opened.

She heard Mollie's excited little voice as she chirped out the events of her day. Sarge, the shepherd mix who accompanied Derek to the clinic each day, came galloping down the hall with an exuberantly wagging tail to greet her, and she cuddled the big dog for a moment before setting his food bowl on the floor and leaving him to eat.

"...'n me 'n Mommy went to the libary 'n we went to the store 'n I taked a nap—"

"You and Kristin," Derek corrected her.

"Yeah." The little girl was completely unfazed. "An' nen I played wif Play-Doh!"

Kristin smiled grimly to herself as she stuffed her work in her briefcase and walked toward the front of the house. Had he thought she was exaggerating about Mollie's new name for her?

Derek still stood in the foyer holding Mollie in his arms. His daughter had his face sandwiched between her two tiny hands as she looked intently into his eyes and Kristin's heart contracted at the sight of the two dark heads so close together. Quietly, she picked up her jacket. "Hi. I just took the meat loaf out so you can have dinner right away."

Derek stared at her, his blue eyes dark and shuttered. "You're not eating with us again?"

"No. I have a board meeting tonight." Since she'd finished college, she'd sat on the animal sanctuary's board of directors.

His eyebrows rose. "That doesn't start until seven. You have plenty of time."

She couldn't hold the eye contact as she started around him, expecting him to move out of her way. But he didn't move, and his broad shoulder was too close to the door for her to pull it open. Taking a deep breath, she met his gaze with a defiant one of her own. "No, thank you. Excuse me."

"Are you ever going to have supper with us again?" He moved aside, but acted as if he hadn't even heard her and his tone was so aggressive she nearly took a step back before she caught herself.

"I don't know," she said cautiously. This angry man wasn't a Derek with whom she was familiar. He was normally one of the most unflappable people she knew. Of course, half the time he walked around in a fog, thinking about something to do with the animals he treated, she thought tenderly. Then she squelched her mental wanderings. Derek was still standing there waiting for an answer. "Probably. Mollie's birthday is coming up in a few months. I'll make something special for her that night."

"*September!* That's three months away." Both she and Mollie jumped when he bellowed. Mollie immediately started to cry, and the anger in his face turned to helpless concern as he rubbed her little back. "I'm sorry, Munchkin. I didn't mean to scare you."

"D-daddy, don't yell at Kristin," Mollie said. She still had tears in her eyes but the little treble voice was firm.

Derek's mouth dropped open. "She sounds just like you!" he said accusingly.

Kristin knew that wasn't a compliment but she wasn't prepared for the hurt that sliced through her. Deb had been sweet and quiet and charming. If she'd ever raised her voice or issued an ultimatum, Kristin couldn't remember it and she sincerely doubted Deb had ever defied Derek in their entire life together. She, Kristin, couldn't be more different from Derek's beloved wife.

Leaning forward, she dropped a kiss on the little girl's forehead. "See you tomorrow, honey," she murmured. The action brought her far too close to Derek and she hastily pulled back and escaped before he could point out any more of her deficiencies.

* * *

Her phone rang just as she was getting out of the shower that evening. She wrapped a bath sheet around her and sprinted for her bedroom, where the closest handset was. "Hello?"

"We have to talk," Derek said without preamble.

"There isn't anything to talk about."

"You know that's not true," he said. "Kris, you can't just cut yourself out of Mollie's life so suddenly. She depends on you."

"It's not like I'm moving to California. I'll be two miles away."

"But she sees you almost every day."

"All right." She threw an exasperated hand into the air even though he couldn't see her. "I'll come by a couple days a week and have lunch with her after you get a new sitter." She made an effort to soften her tone. "That way she won't feel like I'm abandoning her."

"I wish you wouldn't do this." His voice was soft and persuasive.

She wavered, nearly succumbing to the plea. But then she recalled the way he'd refused to take her seriously yesterday. "I have to," she said equally softly. "I need to start living my own life, Derek. And so do you."

"What does that mean?" There was a note of suspicion in his tone now.

She sighed. What could she say that would persuade him to stop trying to change her mind? "We spend far too much of our free time together."

"So?"

"So we each need to learn to live alone."

"Yesterday you wanted to marry me."

"Yes," she said steadily, "I did." If he was trying to get her goat, he was succeeding. "But you made your position crystal-clear so I might as well accept it."

"I think you're punishing me for telling you no."

"I am not!" she said indignantly. "I just think it's time we all moved on. Deb's been gone almost three years, and we've floated along in the same arrangement we had before she died. It can't be good for any of us and if it isn't going to be permanent, then we need to recognize that. I want a family of my own someday and no man is going to be interested in me as long as I'm so involved with you and Mollie." Lordy, she hoped he didn't take that statement at more than face value. She was already feeling humiliated enough without having him know that she had feelings for him.

There was a heavy silence on the line and she held her breath. Derek could barely stand to have his wife's name mentioned; how was he going to react to *that* statement?

Then he sighed. "Maybe you're right," he said quietly. "It isn't fair of me to monopolize you indefinitely. You've been so wonderful with Mollie that it was easy for me to forget you have your own life to live."

"Thank you." She had to work to keep her throat from closing up. This was a poor second-best option if she couldn't have him. It was the hardest thing she'd ever had to do in her entire life. "I have to go. See you Monday."

"Kris?" She loved the way he said her nickname. No one else had ever called her that.

"Yes?"

"I don't want to lose touch. Promise me you won't dump us completely."

She laughed, perilously close to tears again. "I'd never do that. You and Mollie are the only family I have."

There was a small, warm silence.

"'Night," she said.

"'Night." His voice was affectionate.

Slowly, she hung up the phone and sank down on the side of her bed, heedless of the damp towel, fighting back the sobs that tightened her chest.

As she reached for a tissue, the phone rang again. She checked the caller ID, tempted to ignore it, but when she recognized the voice of the treasurer of the animal sanctuary's board, she thought she'd better take it. The time was well past nine, not a usual time for him to be calling. She hoped there wasn't a problem.

Two

She called Derek back moments later.

"Kris," he said patiently before she could get out a word, "I thought we'd finished this discussion." Apparently he'd checked his caller ID as well.

"Don't be an ass. I'm calling about something else." Her voice broke, ruining the sharp retort.

"What's wrong?" His voice changed instantly. "Are you all right?"

She took a deep breath, striving for calm. "Cathie Balisle was killed in a collision an hour ago."

"*What?*" Derek was instantly diverted from their personal exchange. "What happened?"

Cathie Balisle was the executive director of the Appalachian Animal Sanctuary. Kristin's father had hired her when he'd gotten a million-dollar bequest not long after the sanctuary had opened and she'd turned out to be a perfect choice for the job. "Drunk driver," Kristin told him. "Rusty Sheffield just called. I told him I'd call you."

"Man, that's bad news." She could picture him running a hand through his hair like he always did when he was agitated, ruffling the dark waves into disordered spikes. "I can't believe it."

"I know." Her throat felt too tight to speak. Although they hadn't been close on a personal basis, Cathie and she had worked on AAS projects together many times, and Cathie had been her father's choice to head the sanctuary. "All that energy and drive, just—just gone."

Derek exhaled heavily. "What's the board going to do?"

"I doubt anyone's even thought about that yet," she said, "but I imagine we'll advertise immediately. Interview and hire as fast as we possibly can." The sanctuary was a large facility with a big budget and constant management issues. They couldn't afford to be without an executive director.

"Let me know as soon as you hear when the funeral is. We'll get a sitter for Mollie so we both can go." Derek's deep voice was compassionate.

Wryly, she noted that he apparently had forgotten what she'd said about separating their lives, but she didn't have the energy to battle with him right now. "Okay."

"Thanks for calling. Keep me posted." Derek had taken Paul Gordon's seat on the board until Kristin had finished college and had time to fill the vacancy. Although he was no longer directly involved in that end of things he still liked to keep abreast of the sanctuary's agenda.

The following day, Kristin learned that Cathie's funeral was scheduled for two days later at eleven in the morning.

When she called to tell him, Derek said, "I'll close the clinic for a few hours. Sandy says she'll come over to the house and watch Mollie while we're gone."

"Tell her thank you," Kristin offered.

"I'll just bring her over when I pick you up at ten-thirty."

She hesitated, thinking of her new resolve. "That's not necessary."

He was silent for a moment. "This isn't the time for prickly independence, Kris," he said quietly. "We do this kind of stuff together."

Funerals, he meant. *As they'd done first her father's, and then his wife's. Together.* Suddenly, it occurred to her that the funeral of a young woman might be difficult for him. "All right," she said, her heart aching for him.

Kristin hadn't stayed for dinner any night since she'd issued that ultimatum. Despite that, Derek was all too aware that she still made sure there was a hot meal waiting for Mollie and him at the end of the day when he came home.

He used to look forward to getting home, to having

Mollie run into his arms while he and Kristin traded smiles as she babbled about her day. To sitting on the stool in the kitchen with Mollie on his lap while he told Kris about his day, to her reactions to everything from animals he'd been unable to save to owners who thought he was crazy to bill them for certain services. This week, he'd been called out of bed in the middle of the night to try to save a dog who'd been hit by a car while running loose. The dog died, and the owners couldn't understand why he billed them. He'd had to take Mollie to the spare bedroom at the clinic until Kristin arrived to get her. Then he'd had to call his surgical technician to come in, and they had worked for three hours and administered several bags of IV fluids before the dog finally succumbed to shock.

But Kristin hadn't heard that story, because she hadn't stuck around to talk since Tuesday. Dinner was on the table when he arrived and she was out the door before he even had his coat off. He'd eaten alone with Mollie—which wasn't a bad thing, he hastened to assure himself. It was just that he'd gotten used to the adult companionship.

And if he was honest, he missed her. He was actually looking forward to Cathie's funeral today because he would have some time to talk to Kris.

But when he picked her up for the funeral, she was unusually quiet. Despite the warmth of the early June morning, she was wearing a black pantsuit with a matching jacket and her oval face was unreadable. This was probably hitting her hard. Cathie had known

Kris's dad, in a way had been one of the few remaining links to her past.

He held the car door for her and then went around to his own seat. As they drove toward the funeral home, she was still quiet.

"How was your morning?" he asked.

That elicited a brief smile. "Fine. I took Mollie to play with the Mothers of Preschoolers group at the Methodist church. She's in love with Jethrup Sowers's little boy. They walked around holding hands the whole time."

He chuckled. "Sounds like more fun than mine. Three overweight, geriatric dachshunds whose owner doesn't understand why they're having back trouble, a macaw who's plucking her own feathers and a Yorkie with a broken leg."

"How did it get broken?"

"Stepped on."

Silence.

Derek felt like a fidgety fourth-grader again as he braked for a red light. "Has the board spoken at all about hiring someone to—to replace Cathie?" He felt crass, voicing the thought aloud but Cathie had loved the sanctuary and he knew she'd be concerned if she were in their position.

"No. Not yet." Kris was gazing out the window. Her hands lay limply in her lap and without thinking he reached over and put one of his atop them.

The moment he touched her he knew it was a mistake. Dammit! All these years they'd been friends, and ever since she'd said what she'd said, he'd been more aware of her physically than he had any woman since…since he was young. Her hands were warm, her skin silky, and he resisted the fierce urge to smooth his thumb across the tender flesh. If her hands were that silky—*cut it out, Derek.*

Kris hadn't moved a muscle since he'd touched her. Now, she looked down at her lap, where his much larger hand easily covered both her dainty ones. His fingers actually curled around and under hers and he could feel the give of her thigh, soft and very warm, beneath the backs of his fingers.

She lifted her head and looked at him and he felt as if he'd been hit in the stomach, breathless, gasping for air. Her eyes were as green as emeralds sparkling in sunshine, soft and vulnerable, and a bolt of intense sexual attraction shot through him with the unexpected ferocity of a clap of summer thunder.

"Stop it," he said harshly, barely aware of the words. He pulled his hand away as if touching her would blister his skin.

Her eyebrows rose in bewilderment. "Stop what?"

"Stop teasing me." The instant he said it, he knew it was unfair, but he was too stirred up to retreat. In some weird way, he *wanted* to have a rip-roaring fight with her.

"Teasing you?" She repeated the words as if they were in a foreign language. Then he saw fire kindle in her eyes. "Teasing you! I was doing nothing of the kind." She sucked in a breath of outrage. "*You* were the one who touched me!"

"I'm not talking about touching." Although he'd

probably give up the deed to his home if he could put his hands on that yielding, tender flesh again. "I'm talking about the come-hither looks." The light finally changed and he started through the intersection. The church was only two blocks away.

"The…" Her voice trailed off into silence. "What on *earth* is the matter with you? I wouldn't know how to give a 'come-hither look' if my life depended on it."

He was already regretting his words, aware that he wasn't exactly acting rationally, but the steady increase in arousal he was experiencing, a longing that only grew sharper as the tension grew between them, prevented him from admitting it. Staring through the front windshield, he concentrated on his driving.

Beside him, Kristin made a small motion of frustration that he caught in his peripheral vision. "You," she said in a controlled, precise tone, "are a jerk."

And those were the last words spoken. He parked at the church and she was out of the car and stalking across the parking lot before he could come around to get her door. He took long strides to catch up with her although she completely ignored him, signing her name in the register and slipping into a seat near the back of the quiet room. He took the seat beside her, and she made a production out of moving over so that her body didn't brush his.

Hell. What was he going to do about Kristin? *Nothing. She's too young for you.* But ever since she'd mentioned marriage and he'd begun to think of

her as a woman rather than the girl he'd felt responsible for for the past eight years, he hadn't been able
to ignore her lithe figure.

The funeral service began then, and he tuned in
with relief, shoving aside his troubled thoughts. Most
of the board members of the animal sanctuary were
there, as were employees and a lot of other local people who had come to know Cathie through her skill-
ful fund-raising efforts. He'd closed his clinic, and
Faye was there as well, along with several other
members of the staff.

Beside him, he was aware that Kristin was crying
quietly as the minister delivered a touching eulogy.
Fishing in his pocket, he offered her his handkerchief,
but she studiously ignored him and pulled a tissue
from her own pocket. He wanted badly to put his
arm around her and offer her comfort—but he suspected that after the way he'd behaved, she'd chew
off his arm at the shoulder. Instead, all he could do
was watch her from the corner of his eye. He could
practically feel the control she exerted to quiet herself.

By the time the service ended, she was calm again.
They made the short ride to the cemetery in utter
silence and joined the other mourners for the brief
graveside service. Afterward, Kristin stepped forward
to speak briefly to Cathie's parents. He did the same,
but then got caught by one of the animal sanctuary's
board members who asked him in a quiet undertone
if he had any suggestions for a replacement for

Cathie. He shook his head and hurried to catch up with Kris.

As he came up behind her near the car, he realized she was crying again. She wept silently, her slender shoulders shaking and he stood there awkwardly, wondering what to do. He clenched his fists to prevent himself from reaching out and touching her. But after a moment, he couldn't take the quiet sobbing anymore and he raised his arms and slipped them around her, pulling her close.

She burrowed against him instantly like a small creature seeking shelter from harm, her arms tightening around his waist. But almost as instantly she stiffened in his arms. "I'm not teasing you." Her voice was muffled in his chest.

A wave of tenderness surged through him and he stroked a hand down her back. "I know. I'm sorry for that...earlier. I was just in a filthy mood."

She didn't reply, but her body relaxed against his, and she let him hold her.

It was a mistake again, touching her, but at least this time he was prepared for the rush of awareness that tightened his gut and made his whole body feel hot and tingly. He bent his head and brushed his lips over the crown of her head. "I'm sorry. I know you really liked Cathie."

She nodded. "I did." He could feel her warm breath through his summer-weight shirt and an involuntary shiver chased down his spine. "Daddy chose her, you know."

He nodded, understanding her grief. "I know. Brings it all back, doesn't it?"

She nodded.

Over her head, he saw Faye walking along the edge of the narrow road that wound through the cemetery. As she picked her way around his car, her gaze met his, and she gave him a smug, knowing smile.

He stifled a ridiculous urge to stick his tongue out at her and helped Kristin into the car. As he drove her home again, he clung to denial: a marriage between them was a ludicrous thought. She was young, fresh. He was a widower with a child. Their personalities didn't mesh in any way as his had with Deb's. They'd fight. It would never work.

The next day was her Saturday to volunteer at the animal sanctuary. She dressed in baggy khaki shorts and a comfortably oversize T-shirt, grabbed a toaster pastry and reached for her car keys. The whole time she was getting ready, she was worrying at the problem of finding a new executive director, mentally writing an ad to place.

But when she opened her door, Faye Proctor stood on the other side. Kristin nearly barreled into her, jolting to a halt with a gasp of surprise.

Faye put a hand to her throat and chuckled. "Lordy, you startled me!"

"You startled me, too." She opened the door and gestured for Faye to enter. "Come on in. I have to help at Appalachian today but I have a few minutes. What's up?"

Faye sank onto the couch in Kristin's small living room and Kristin took a seat opposite her. When their eyes met, Faye's usually cheerful gaze was surprisingly sober. "Derek told me about your suggestion last week."

Great. If a person could vanish in a puff of smoke, Kristin fervently wished it would happen right now. This very moment. She squeezed her eyes tightly shut, feeling heat creep into her face, but when she opened them, Faye was still there, gazing patiently at her.

"Oh," said Kristin weakly. "That…rat."

Faye laughed. "I betcha 'rat' isn't the word you really want to use!"

"Well, no," she said, smiling a little, "it's not."

"I don't mean to pry," Faye assured her. "The thing is, I agree with you, honey."

Kristin stared at the older woman, speechless. She did?

"Dr. Mahoney's a great boss," Faye said, "and I love working for him. But it's been hard to watch him shut himself away from everything but that little girl since dear Debbie died. You're all that's kept him from folding his tents completely—"

"I don't know about that," Kristin interrupted.

"I do," Faye said. "You make him eat and go to work. You help with his housework and do his laundry. You've raised Miss Mollie, don't think you haven't."

"That may be true, but as Derek pointed out to me, those aren't reasons to get married." She shrugged, trying to stave off the hurt the memory produced. They'd patched up their disagreement, if that was what that odd, charged exchange in which he'd accused her of teasing him had been, but there had been an uncomfortable strain between them that had lingered until she'd thanked him for the ride and slid out of his car.

Faye snorted. "That man can't see his nose on his own darn face. Don't you pay him any mind."

Kristin tilted her head. "What do you mean?"

"Any fool can see you care about Dr. Mahoney," said Faye.

"Is it that obvious?" She was dismayed.

"No, no," said Faye hastily. "But I've known you since you were a little girl and I've never seen you look at a man the way you look at Derek when he isn't looking back."

Kristin felt herself flushing. "So?" She didn't mean to be rude. She'd known Faye long enough to know the older woman wouldn't take offense.

"So you've never listened to him before," Faye said, grinning. "You aren't going to start now, are you?"

Well. She had a point. But still… "Yes." She made her voice firm. "I'm not going to live the rest of my life wishing for something I can't have. If Derek doesn't want me, I'm going to open myself to other possibilities."

"You mean other men?" Faye's eyes were wide.

Kristin nodded.

"Don't be hasty, honey. You dragged him back

from the edge of climbing into that grave with Deb,'' Faye reminded her. "He didn't know what was good for him, and he still doesn't.''

"But…'' She was at a loss as to how to handle this strange conversation. "How am I supposed to…what can I do when he says—''

"Feminine wiles." Faye smiled meaningfully. She tapped a brown shopping bag she'd brought in and set on the floor beside her. "I've got a few things in here that my daughter Carlie can't wear since she had the baby. We're going to make you look more like a woman."

"More like a woman?'' She fingered the mass of shining curls that fell over her shoulder. "I don't think I exactly resemble a guy."

"No," Faye agreed. "You sure don't. We're just going to remind Dr. Mahoney a little bit."

"How?" Kristin asked suspiciously. "I don't want to have to wear a bunch of makeup—''

"Honey, with that face and hair you don't need makeup!'' Faye stood up and shook out something in a pretty shade of teal that she'd pulled from the bag. "But your clothes are another matter."

"I like to be comfortable." What did she mean about the face and hair? The face was too pale, even if she did have pretty eyes, and her hair…the color was nice, but the wild curls refused to be tamed. If she cut it short, it would only form a frizzy halo, so she wore it long and usually braided it or pulled it back.

"You like to *hide*," Faye corrected. "You won't

be uncomfortable in these things, but you'll be noticed, that's for sure."

The teal fabric was a slinky knit dress, sleeveless and scoop-necked. There were several little sleeveless tops, a pair of well-worn jeans and a denim skirt that didn't look big enough to cover her butt.

"The dress is for evening," Faye told her. "Try this stuff. Once you've gotten used to it, we'll go shopping and get you some things of your own to match the new you."

"I can't afford to go shopping." That was true. Her father had poured all his money into establishing Appalachian and had been heavily in debt when he died. Although at seventeen she technically still had been a minor, it had never occurred to her to default on the loans he had made. The money she'd gotten from Derek for the house and the practice had gone a long way toward erasing what she owed, but she still had a heavy schedule of loan payments to make for another year. She could hardly wait until the loan was paid off. Then she could start saving for a house of her own.

"Secondhand shops and Goodwill," Faye said. "I've gotten some great stuff there." She shoved the bag into Kristin's hands. "Now go try on these things."

Faye was a force of nature when she was on a mission and Kristin knew better than to argue. If she hurried, she wouldn't be too late.

Everything fit like a dream. And that was a problem. She was used to wearing loose, baggy clothing.

She couldn't even remember the last time she'd worn a skirt and she felt disconcertingly exposed. Even to church, she wore one of two trouser suits she'd had for years.

"I can't go out in public in this," she said as she came out of the half bath off her small kitchen. "This" was the teal dress. It was deceptively simple on a hanger, but on a body…she was afraid she might just be illegal.

"You look terrific!" Faye crowed, walking all around her. "What's the matter?"

"It's…" She motioned vaguely. "Too revealing."

"It's modest compared to what some girls are wearing these days. Go try the rest."

Faye approved each of the other items, but when Kristin attempted to change back into her own clothing, the older woman shook her head. "Just wear that today."

Kristin looked down at herself. She was wearing the jean skirt with a spring-green camisole top. The top had a tiny drawstring bow made of ribbon at the rounded neckline, and ribbon was laced through the straps as well. The only saving grace was that she could still wear her bra. "Isn't it a little bare?"

"No. It's summery and feminine. That skirt looks a whole lot better on you than those baggy drawers you've been wearing. And wear your hair down." Faye walked around behind her and slipped the loose fabric twist free.

"But it gets in my way."

"Then cut it."

"No!" Kristin put a protective hand to her head. Then she saw Faye's lips twitch and she smiled reluctantly. "Okay. I'll wear it down. It *is* pretty like this, isn't it?"

"It's beautiful, honey," Faye said gently. "And so are you. Now go to Appalachian and enjoy the compliments you get."

"All right," she said doubtfully. She probably wouldn't see many people today, anyway. What was the harm? "I'll try it today. But I'm not promising any drastic wardrobe changes."

"It's a deal," said Faye.

"But Faye...I'm not doing this for Derek." On that point she was certain. "I'm doing it for me. If he's not interested, maybe I'll find someone who is."

The older woman just nodded and smiled. "Either way, you're bound to get some reaction."

But from whom? Kristin said farewell to Faye and climbed into her small truck, hoping she wouldn't be too late. She did whatever was needed, but most often she worked the desk because Cathie said she was so good with the public.

Her eyes closed briefly in sadness as she thought of Cathie. And then they sprang open again. *The public!* How had she forgotten? Today was Summerfest, an annual fund-raising and public relations event the animal sanctuary held each June. They'd considered postponing it after Cathie died, but it was too big an event. And in any case, Cathie wouldn't have wanted that. Summerfest had been her brainstorm originally. The best way to honor her, the board members had

decided, was to carry out the event she had organized.

There would be a skillion visitors, not to mention
media attendees, all over the public areas. And here
she was, dressed like a refugee from an 'NSYNC
concert.

Three

––––

It was a beautiful day for Summerfest. The sun shone brightly but there was a hint of breeze and the temperature hovered in the upper seventies just before noon. As Derek lifted Mollie from her car seat, he noticed that there was a sizable crowd milling around the sanctuary parking lot, where many different kinds of booths and activities were set up beneath nearby shade trees.

In the center of the lot, a local dog club had set up an agility course and members were demonstrating their dogs' skills on various pieces of equipment. A schedule prominently posted near the refreshment tables displayed times for demonstrations of such varied animal events as guide dog puppy raisers, a bird breeder with her talking parrots, a detection dog team who searched for drugs and a woman who rescued orphaned bear cubs. Pony rides were offered in a nearby meadow as well as guided tours of the sanctuary.

Derek had just set Mollie on her feet when she gave a piercing squeal. "Mom-meeeee!" He grabbed her just as she nearly made a mad dash across the parking lot.

"Whoa, there, chickadee."

"Down, Daddy!" His daughter was a wriggling bundle of feminine outrage. "I wanna go see Mommy."

He tried to keep the frustration he felt from his voice as he said, "Kristin's not your mommy, Mollie. She's our friend."

He glanced at the crowd, his pulse quickening, but he didn't see her, and he decided Mollie must have been mistaken. But as he reached the edge of the asphalt where the frenzy of the celebration was in full swing, his gaze caught a flash of white blond curls. He lifted his head in time to see Kristin standing in front of the animal sanctuary office with two of the board members.

Only…*was* it Kristin? She wore a skirt—Kris *never* wore skirts. And not just any skirt. A short denim skirt that hugged her slender hips and showed an indecent amount of long, bare leg. With it she wore an equally skimpy little tank top of some clingy fabric that displayed feminine curves he'd had no real idea she possessed. Well, he supposed he had, but he'd just never thought about her that way…until last week. Now it seemed to be *all* he could think about.

He surveyed her again, his pulse kicking up a notch. Good lord. It was a wonder every man in the place hadn't had a heart attack if she'd been walking around like that all morning. Her hair was down— what was with that?—spilling down her back and curling around her shoulders like a caressing hand. Loose tendrils floated in the breeze. As he watched, a strand wafted across the face of the man to her left and he caught it with a smile, tugging playfully as Kristin tried to restrain the rest.

The half-breathless feeling inside him vanished and he felt like snarling.

Mollie tugged at his hand again. "Wanna go see Kristin."

"Okay." He released her hand and followed more slowly, watching as his daughter made a beeline through the crowd. The buzz of voices around him made it impossible to hear, but he knew the moment Kristin saw Mollie. Her pretty face lit up in a spontaneous expression of delight and she knelt, stretching out her arms.

In the instant before Mollie ran into her embrace, he couldn't help noticing how the position pulled Kristin's skirt high up her thighs, exposing a tantalizing triangle of shadow between her legs. He couldn't see panties, but he might as well have been able to.

A surge of arousal so strong he actually stopped in his tracks slammed into him. God, she was lovely.

Why hadn't he noticed before? *You did,* he reminded himself. *You've always thought Paul's daughter would grow into a beautiful woman someday.*

The trouble was, "someday" had apparently arrived while he wasn't looking.

He forced himself to start forward again, trying to get his raging hormones under control. The last thing he needed was for Kristin to think he had the hots for her. It would totally destroy the friendly family relationship they'd always had.

Yeah. Like you didn't do that when you accused her of teasing you. What an idiot.

"Dr. Mahoney. Glad you could come by." The older of the two men still flanking Kristin thrust out a hand. Walker Glave was a local attorney who served as the sanctuary board's president and donated his time when they had legal issues with wills and trusts to work out.

"I wouldn't miss it." Derek shook the hand, then squatted down in front of his daughter and Kristin. "Sorry. She saw you the moment we arrived."

"Don't be sorry. I'm delighted to see my Miss Mollie." She spoke to the child rather than to him, tweaking her nose playfully as Mollie giggled.

Derek leaned forward a little, speaking in an undertone. "You might consider changing that position before every man here gets a look beneath your skirt."

Her gaze flew to his as her eyes widened, and a red patch of color appeared in each cheek. Hastily, she stood, lifting Mollie into her arms. "Come on,

Mols. Let's go get some lemonade and let Daddy visit for a while.''

"Not too long,'' he said to her back as she started away. "I'm serious about not monopolizing your day.'' She didn't answer, but he was sure she'd heard him, and he made himself a mental note to try to keep track of the time. That wasn't his strong suit.

"Hey, Doc.'' The younger, taller man extended a hand. An insurance salesman with a busy office in Quartz Forge, Rusty Sheffield currently was the treasurer of the board. "Good to see you. We miss having you on the board.'' He turned to eye Kris's back view as she walked away. "Although having Kristin there isn't exactly a hardship.''

"Kristin may not be on the board if she accepts the offer,'' Walker said.

"What offer?'' Derek told himself he only was annoyed by Rusty's leering expression because of the promise he'd made her father always to look out for her.

"We've asked her to consider temporarily filling the executive director's position,'' Rusty said.

Derek was too surprised to speak.

"What do you think about it?'' Rusty pressed.

"I—ah, I don't know.'' He made an effort to gather his thoughts.

"We'd be taking away his baby-sitter,'' the older board member said. "What do you *expect* him to say?''

"No, it's not that,'' he said hastily. "It's just that I never thought of Kristin as…''

"Neither did we," Walker said. "But the minute someone mentioned her, we couldn't think of a single reason why we wouldn't want her. She'll be terrific."

Derek couldn't think of a single reason *he* wouldn't want her, either, but he doubted they were speaking of the same thing. God, why couldn't he seem to get his mind off sex today? Slowly, he nodded as he forced his attention back to the men and considered the idea. Why hadn't she talked to him about it? He winced inwardly, recalling again his behavior the day of the funeral. He knew exactly why, and he forced himself to consider her in terms of the position. "She'll do an excellent job for you."

"Temporarily," said Walker. "Just for a few months until we can interview and hire the right person. You know that handling a nonprofit of this size is no easy task."

"If Kristin does take the job," Rusty said, "we'd like you to come back and fill her spot on the board. Other than Kristin, you're the closest thing to Paul Gordon's family, and you knew his wishes."

"I'll have to think about it," he said, "but thank you for the offer."

"Dr. Mahoney!" A chubby woman in a pink, flowered dress sailed toward them. "How nice to see you. I wanted to thank you again for all you did for Apricot. Her allergies seem to be under control now and her coat is growing in as beautifully as it was before."

Derek pasted on a smile and turned to his client. The only trouble with being a vet in a small town was that his clients were everywhere. And they all assumed he was waiting breathlessly to hear about their pet's latest health crises. He loved animals, and he loved his job, but it surely would be nice to go out in public sometime and have someone ask his opinion on who should be baseball's MVP or how his newest woodcarving effort was coming.

Two hours later, he was still being held captive by clients talking about their pets when he heard Kristin's voice. "Derek? It's time to eat." She smiled at the couple currently regaling him with tales of their Jack Russell. "Sorry. I'm the spoilsport who makes sure Dr. Mahoney takes a break every now and then."

"Thank you," he said beneath his breath as he followed her to a table where apparently she'd already gotten two plates of food. "In my nightmares sometimes, I'm surrounded by people telling pet stories and I can't get away."

She smiled, swiping back a curling lock of hair that the breeze had caught. "I thought you were starting to look a little desperate."

He sat gratefully, checking his heaping plate. "Yum. Deviled eggs and brownies. You must have been near the front of the line. The eggs are always gone by the time I get there." He glanced around, parental unease rearing its head. "Where's Mollie?"

She pointed to the wide grassy yard where a group of teenagers were organizing children's games and he spotted his daughter. "One of the girls is keeping an eye on Mollie for a little while."

"Thanks." He waited until she took a seat beside him, then began to eat, realizing only as he surveyed the rest of the items on his plate that Kristin had chosen just about every one of his favorites from the buffet tables. A different sort of uneasiness snaked through him. Did she really know him that well? He had a sneaking suspicion she did.

"Did Walker and Rusty tell you about the offer they made me?" Her voice broke into his thoughts.

He nodded. "They did. What do you think?"

She hesitated. "I don't know. It's temporary, and this is a good time of year for me, since my accounting work won't really pick up until winter sets in. I think it would be challenging and interesting, but…"

"But what?"

She shrugged. "I'm just not sure." She set down her spoon and looked at him. "Do you think I should take it?"

"Do I *want* you to take it or do I *think* you should take it?" He forced himself to grin. "I don't want you to take it because you've been a terrific babysitter and Mollie depends on you. But since you've already said you're leaving anyway, yes, I think you should take it. You're organized, creative, good with people and budget-conscious. I think you'd be great at it."

She looked a little stunned. "Thank you," she finally said.

When she didn't speak again, he glanced at her around a mouthful of brownie. "Did I say something wrong?'' he asked. Heaven only knew what was going through that convoluted brain of hers.

"No." She smiled, delicately licking brownie icing from the tip of one finger with a pink tongue. "It's just…well, you're not big on compliments. It's nice to know you think I'm so capable."

He didn't answer her. Hell, he barely heard her. Every cell in his body was focused on that sweet little tongue as she finished her brownie and licked the rest of the icing from her fingers. God, what would he give to have that tongue licking *him*.

He was still watching her when she picked up her napkin and wiped her fingers. She glanced at him. "Are you…finished?" Her voice stuttered and faded as their eyes met. And held.

They stared across the table at each other and he knew from the rising awareness in her eyes that she recognized the hunger he couldn't hide. Finally, she tore her gaze from his and hastily began to gather plates and utensils together. "We'd better clean up and make space for someone else."

He put out a hand and caught her wrist in a loose, yet unbreakable grip. "Kris."

She stilled.

"You look pretty today." He hadn't intended to say the words, but he found he wasn't sorry he'd spoken.

"Th-thank you."

She'd never made much effort with her clothes and looks before. Despite the fact that she was a truly lovely girl, she'd camouflaged herself so well that she'd gone virtually unnoticed by men. But since she'd begun her campaign to get his attention, he figured she'd decided to use her assets—and as far as he was concerned, she'd done a hell of a job. "Any special reason you dressed up?" he asked with a smile.

But the moment he spoke, her eyes went flat. The warmth and attraction in her gaze vanished so completely it was as if it had never existed. She tugged at her wrist until he let go. "I don't want to be an old maid," she said quietly. "From now on, I'm not going to hide when a man shows interest in me, and I'm not going to hide myself, either."

He didn't like the sound of that and he frowned. "A man like Rusty Sheffield? Did he ask you out?"

She shrugged. "It's really not your business."

The hell it wasn't. "He's too immature for you."

Her eyebrows rose. "He's four years older than I am! That's hardly immature."

"He's been through practically every single woman in town. Do you want to be the subject of the weekly barbershop gossip?"

"It would be better than never being noticed at all," she shot back. She looked angry now. "Rusty's too immature and you're too old. You're not leaving me much of a window of opportunity here, Derek."

He wanted to shake her. He wanted to grab her and kiss her until she quit talking, and the only thing that saved her—and him—was the table between them. "I just don't want to see you get hurt." It was part of the truth, at least.

"Oh, get over yourself," she snapped. "You haven't been my guardian for eight years now." And before he could speak again, she snatched up a handful of dirty dishes and stalked off toward the trash can, her long legs eating up the ground as she moved away from him.

Wearily, he ran a hand through his hair. What was the matter with him? Every time he was around her these days, he seemed to provoke an argument. He really hadn't intended to make her mad. He just didn't want her going out with some jerk that might use her and hurt her.

Right. You want her for yourself and you just can't admit it.

There's nothing to admit, he defended himself staunchly to the inner voice that shouted for his attention. *She's like my family. I have to look out for her.*

Since when does looking out for her include drooling over her legs and her lips?

He didn't have an answer for that one.

The last few weeks of June were hectic.

Kristin informed him on the Monday after Summerfest that the day care right down the street from his practice had an opening in Mollie's age group, and that she could start as soon as he visited and filled out the paperwork.

Hell, she even filled it out and brought it to him, then stood over him while he signed his name and date in the appropriate places. She couldn't have made it clearer that she was eager to ditch Mollie and him.

It wasn't that he objected to day care. In fact, he'd been reluctant to leave Mollie alone with a stranger in the house all day anyway. At day care, she'd be with experienced professionals and she'd have other kids to play with.

But still…he hadn't said any of that to Kristin before she shoved those papers down his throat.

She started working at the animal sanctuary on Wednesday, the same day he dropped Mollie off at day care for the first time. Mollie seemed happy enough, and he went to work feeling less guilty than he'd expected.

The feeling lasted until he picked her up in the evening, and found her in one of the helper's arms, sobbing her little heart out.

"Daddy." She scrambled for him the moment he entered the room and he bent to lift her into his arms, feeling his own heart crack as he surveyed her tear-stained cheeks and the thumb in her mouth, something she rarely did anymore unless she was really tired or stressed.

"Hi, chickadee." He tried to inject a positive note into his voice. "Did you have a good time today?"

She shook her head slowly from side to side.

"Aw, Mollie, we had a lot of fun this morning!" The aide, a relentlessly cheerful older woman, beamed as she came over to address them. "You'll have to tell Daddy about finger painting and our Richie Raccoon story time. And don't forget tomorrow is Share It Day. Bring something blue from home to tell your friends about during Share It.''

Blue?

The woman smiled at him. ''We're working on the color blue this week, so everyone is bringing in a blue Share It.''

He nodded. ''What happened…?'' He indicated his daughter, who had wrapped her arms around his neck and laid her head on his shoulder, and just that fast, was sound asleep.

The woman's smile wilted a little. ''She didn't nap today. She kept saying she needed her hair. Is there a special doll or blanket she sleeps with?''

Derek shook his head, puzzled. ''No, not really.''

''Well, don't worry too much,'' the aide advised. ''The first few days are always an adjustment for the little ones. I'm sure she'll be fine in no time.''

Mollie didn't wake up even when he put her in her car seat, and he had to work to get her awake enough to eat dinner. She livened up around bath time and began to chatter about her day, and when bedtime rolled around, she was still wide-awake and totally wired.

When Kristin called, he was at his wit's end.

''Hi,'' she said, and he could hear a cool note in her voice. ''I just called to see how Mollie's first day went. I promised to stop in at lunch a few days a week but I figured I'd better wait a day or two until she gets into a routine and doesn't think I've come to pick her up.''

He sighed. ''It didn't go so well.''

"Oh, no. What happened?" As Mollie squealed happily in the background, Kristin said, "What is she doing still up? She needs to be in bed by eight or she'll be awful tomorrow."

"I know," he said defensively, "but she wouldn't nap for them today and she fell asleep on the way home and now she's got her second wind."

Kristin was silent and he could feel the censure right through the receiver. But when she spoke, she didn't sound like she was condemning him. "Did they say why she wouldn't sleep?"

"Something about needing her hair," he reported. "I don't get it. She doesn't sleep with a blanket or a doll—"

"It's *my* hair," Kristin said flatly. "Shoot. I'm sorry. I never thought to tell you. I used to sit with her in my lap after lunch. I'd read a story and then put her down for her nap. She takes a handful of my hair and brushes it back and forth over her cheek and it puts her right to sleep."

Oh, man. Now that she'd said it, he knew exactly what she meant. He'd seen Mollie doing it on more than one occasion but since he'd never had trouble getting her to sleep for him, he'd never connected the dots. "Well, hell," he said in disgust. "What am I going to tell the day care? I don't guess you'd be able to—"

"I can't go over there every day and put her down for her nap," Kristin said briskly. "Even if they'd allow it, I'm not going to have time. The sanctuary is in an uproar right now and I'm going to have work coming out my ears.''

"Sorry," he said immediately, meaning it. "I didn't really expect you to. Any suggestions?''

There was a short silence. "I'll tell you what," she said. "How about if I meet you there in the morning. I'll let Mollie cut a lock of my hair and we'll tie it up and keep it in a bag so that at nap time she can get it out and keep it with her.''

"You can't cut your hair!" He was truly shocked.

She laughed. "Just a little piece from underneath. Derek, you know how much hair I have. I'll never even know it's gone.''

Oh, he knew exactly. Hadn't he been having dreams of that moon-silvered mass of curls sliding over his body? Belatedly, he realized she was awaiting a response. "Uh, that would be terrific," he said. "If you're sure you don't mind.''

"Not at all." Her voice was brisk again. "See you in the morning.''

She was as good as her word the following day, although he was disappointed that she didn't linger a little longer. She was wearing jeans today with a T-shirt, but they weren't the baggy pants she'd once worn. These hugged her curves and emphasized the length of her legs. The shirt, too, was different. He was used to seeing her in large, floppy shirts—this one fit her snugly.

"Don't you have to dress up a little for work?" he asked her.

"Not today." She jingled her car keys, clearly

anxious to go. "I don't have any appointments today and one of the kennel staff broke an arm yesterday, so until we find a temporary replacement, I may have to help out in the kennels." She grinned. "One thing's for sure—I'll never get bored doing the same old thing at this job."

Her words bothered him. "I'm sorry if baby-sitting was—"

"No, no," she said in exasperation. "I wasn't comparing the two. I only meant this is nothing like having a dry old accounting practice all day every day."

He felt better instantly, and as she walked back to her car, he couldn't stop himself from checking out her back view. Damn. He shook his head, his good mood evaporating. She was going to have men all over her.

Aside from thoughts of the way Kristin's hair swayed just above her heart-shaped behind in the tight jeans, he had a good day at the clinic. When he went to pick up Mollie, the aide reported that she'd had a wonderful nap.

They fell into a passable routine. Kristin called every few days to see how Mollie was and he knew from Mollie's chatter that she was stopping by the day care, but he hadn't seen her in almost two weeks, since she'd stopped to drop off a lock of her hair.

God, he missed her. He missed the indulgent glances they used to share at Mollie's antics. He missed coming home to a lighted house and a hot meal, but even more, he missed coming home to her warm smile and the lazy discussions they'd had over dinner. He missed drying dishes and ducking when she flicked a towel at him, he missed seeing the tender way she kissed Mollie's temple, the way she always took the time to kneel and rub Sarge's furry belly.

It was ridiculous. He'd allowed himself to slide along after Deb's death, had allowed Kristin to do far too much to hold his family together, had gotten far too accustomed to having her in his life. Now he hated being alone without adult companionship. Without *female* companionship, and one particular female at that.

When the phone rang on the last Friday in June, he leaped for it, his spirits lifting as he glanced at the clock. Nine in the evening. Kristin usually called about this time to see how they were doing.

"Hello?"

"Hi. Can I stop over?"

"Sure. Right now?" *Sure!* He'd love to see her.

"Yes. I have something I need to talk to you about." Her voice sobered him. She didn't sound happy, and he racked his brain, wondering what was wrong. Had he done something to upset her?

He had his answer in five minutes. He was watching for her car and he opened the door before she even got to the porch.

"Hi."

"Hi." She stepped into the kitchen and she set down a large, handled file box. "I need your opinion on something."

"Sure." He turned a chair backward and straddled it, facing her. "Sit down and talk to me." He couldn't prevent the smile that crept across his face. "It's good to see you."

She smiled back. "It's good to see you, too." The moment lingered, but before it could turn into anything else, she shook herself and reached for the box of files she'd brought along. "I think we may have a problem at the sanctuary."

"What kind of problem?" He could probably deal with anything that came up. He was familiar with personnel issues, scheduling, all the things that went on in his office—

"Derek," she said, "I think something's wrong with the budget numbers. There's a discrepancy in the books."

"A discrepancy?" He knew all about balancing budgets, but so did she, so why would she come to him about something so mundane?

"Missing money." She swallowed, and as he realized she was upset, her words began to assume meaning.

"As in, a *deliberate* discrepancy?"

She shrugged. "I don't know. But it's hard to imagine that half a million dollars going missing is an accident."

"Half a million." He was too shocked to conceal it. "Five hundred thousand dollars? Where'd it go?"

"If I knew that, it wouldn't be a discrepancy, would it?" Her voice was just the slightest bit sarcastic. Immediately, she said, "I'm sorry. I know how you feel. It's difficult to believe. When I first found it, I went over every column of the books.'' She tapped the stack of files in the box. "It went out, largely in small untraceable sums, but it never came back in again.''

He still couldn't grasp it. "Are you telling me you think Cathie took it?''

"I don't know what to think.'' Her voice was anguished. "But that's what it's looking like.''

"Good God.'' He sat back, and a heavy silence fell. Finally, he stirred. "Well, what do we do? We can't ask her,'' he muttered.

"No.'' Kristin sounded close to tears. "But I absolutely don't want any hint of this to get out and accusations to fly unless we're completely certain that it's really missing and that Cathie had something to do with it.'' She sniffed. "She loved the sanctuary. I can't believe she would embezzle from us.''

"Kris, honey, don't cry.'' Without thinking, he rose from his chair and went to her, drawing her up and into his arms. "Let's double-check everything. Maybe there's some explanation you just missed. You know how it is when you're too close to the numbers.''

She nodded into his chest. "Maybe that's it.'' Her arms tightened around his waist. "Thanks. I knew you'd help.''

"We'll figure it out together,'' he soothed. "You know you can come to me with anything.'' She felt soft and feminine in his arms, her body warm and giving against his, and without letting himself think about whether or not it was wise or smart, he put a finger beneath her chin and tilted her face up to his. "God, Kris, I've missed you so much."

And then her hands were sliding up into his hair and he set his lips on hers, his whole body coming alive to the feel of hers as he tightened his arms and pulled her more fully to him.

Four

It was the kind of kiss she'd dreamed of during countless lonely nights. Derek's arms were around her, bringing her close enough to feel the contours of his strong male frame. One was wrapped around her waist, the other engulfed her shoulders and she could feel his large palms pressing against her back.

She wasn't short, but Derek made her feel tiny and fragile. His dark head blotted out the light as he bent to her and his shoulders seemed a mile wide. His arms and chest were hard and roped with muscle from both his weekly workouts and the hours he spent on the larger animals in his practice. In a town as small as Quartz Forge, a vet couldn't be simply a small-animal vet or an avian vet. Derek handled all the animals, farm, pet and other, that came his way.

His mouth—oh, dear heavens, his mouth! His kiss wasn't tentative, though at first it was sweet and undemanding, his lips caressing and clinging, nibbling at her lower lip and gently sucking it into his mouth. But she wasn't capable of hiding her feelings where he was concerned and when he recognized her response, he teased her lips apart and sought out her tongue, gently flirting with her until his kiss grew deep and sure, his tongue drawing hers into a steady thrust and retreat that echoed the motions of his hips against hers.

She'd run her fingers up the back of his neck when he'd first touched her. Now she spread them wide, cradling his skull as he bent her backward over one arm with the force of his kiss.

His fingers flexed, kneading her waist and she hung in his arms as he melded their hips together. He was heavy and hard against her and she thrilled to the exquisite pleasure of knowing she was the woman who'd gotten him into such a state. Her own body was swollen, throbbing, driving her to move against him, to relieve the breath-stealing intense delight toward which she was steadily spiraling.

But then she became aware of a change in position. Derek was lifting her more upright, and his mouth was gentling, slowing, the contained ferocity of his kisses giving way to calmer, lighter ones as he withdrew. He didn't let her go completely, still loosely encircling her waist, and she allowed her hands to slide down to his chest, suddenly feeling a ridiculous but undeniable shyness, and she couldn't meet his gaze.

"Kris?" His voice was husky and he cleared his throat.

"Yes?" Slowly she lifted her head and made eye contact.

He was smiling, a wry lopsided expression. "I, ah, don't know what to say."

She dared a small smile of her own. "Let's not say anything."

He sighed, his chest rising and falling beneath her hands. "I can't do that, and you know it."

She sighed, too. "Mr. Have-It-All-Laid-Out. You're right—you can't do it."

A frown touched his face and his eyes clouded. "You know me so well...."

"That bothers you?"

He hesitated. "No."

"But you wish you hadn't kissed me." Her euphoria had fled. He didn't have to say it; she read it in his eyes. Hurt sliced through her, even deeper than before. Now she knew what Heaven could be. Having it vanish right before her eyes was hell.

"Yes. No. I don't know!" He threw up his hands and moved away from her, pacing in the familiar way he always did when he was agitated. "I need some time to work out my feelings, to decide what to do—"

"Don't get yourself in a panic, Derek." She kept her voice flat and even, containing tears through sheer willpower as she slid the files back into the box.

"I'm not asking anything of you. Nothing has to change."

He stared at her, his face growing dark. "The hell it doesn't."

"Don't swear at me. I'm just trying to keep you from guilting yourself to death!" Now her voice was sharp with exasperation but doggone it, he was just so darn *dense*. "It was only a kiss."

"Was it?" He stepped forward as she backed toward the door, and suddenly he wasn't safe, familiar Derek anymore. He was a stranger, a stranger with hot, exciting questions in his eyes, a man to whom she felt an overwhelming sexual attraction. He snagged the lapels of her blouse, and hauled her close to him again.

They stared at each other for a moment, the silence thick and charged with tension.

"Things have changed," he said in a low, intense voice. "I just have to figure out what to do about you."

She hated the way he made her sound like a problem he had to take care of and her temper flared again. "There's nothing to figure out," she said, taking his wrists and tugging his hands away, aware that she was only free because he'd allowed it. "You don't make decisions about how you feel. It just happens. Or it doesn't."

She turned the doorknob but he put his hand on the door, holding it closed for a moment. "I need some time to think about you," he said. "About us."

Her heart leaped, but she squashed the blossom of

feeling. How could he not recognize what they had? What they could have? And why on earth did she want a man who had to *think* before deciding how he felt about her?

"There is no us," she said, "and if you imagine I'm going to sit home waiting while you dissect your feelings and decide whether or not I might be allowed to fit into your life, you are seriously mistaken." Her voice was shaking and tears were threatening to spill as she wrestled the door out of his hand and escaped into the night.

Another week passed and the Fourth of July loomed.

Derek was dreading the holiday this year. He and Deb and Kristin had gone to the fireworks together ever since they'd known each other, and after Deb died, they'd kept the tradition going for Mollie. Last year, they'd taken a picnic meal in to the school across from the field where the fireworks display was held. They'd gotten a good spot high on the hill, played with water pistols and read stories until dusk, and then laid on their backs on the blanket—with Mollie between them—and watched the celebration.

This year, who knew how the evening would go?

He hadn't talked to Kristin since she'd slammed out of his house last week after that kiss that had turned his world upside down. She hadn't called for advice or support on her concerns about the money problem at the shelter, and she hadn't even called in the evening to see how Mollie was. The day-care ladies told him she'd been in several times to have lunch or read a story to Mollie, so at least he knew she hadn't abandoned both of them.

Day care. It was going well and after that first disastrous day the transition hadn't been as bad as he'd anticipated. But it still wasn't working very well. They liked the children to be picked up by five-thirty. Six o'clock was the latest they would stretch, and those hours just didn't work for him. The clinic was open two nights a week until seven, which meant he wasn't done until seven-thirty at the very earliest.

When Kristin had kept Mollie, she had gone ahead and fed his daughter earlier and then eaten with him while they talked about their days and Mollie played around the kitchen. Now, he had to have Faye or Sandy run over and pick up Mollie and keep her at the clinic until he was done. They fed her snacks to keep her from getting cranky, so by the time he could get her home and fix dinner, she wasn't hungry anymore. And she usually was cranky anyway.

No, it wasn't working very well. He needed flexibility. And he was beginning to fully appreciate just how flexible his arrangement with Kristin had been. He'd advertised for a nanny and had three people to interview over the next few days, but even with that, he doubted he was going to be completely satisfied with the new arrangement. Kris had made his life so easy she'd spoiled him for anyone else.

He eyed the phone. It was the second of July already, and he'd been waiting for Kristin to call to firm up their plans for the Fourth. But she hadn't called, and he had the feeling she wasn't going to. Well, he could afford to be generous, he decided, picking up the receiver. *He* wasn't the one who'd stalked off in a huff.

And what the heck had that been all about anyway? He hadn't stopped thinking about that kiss all week. Or his reaction to it. Or the way she'd reacted, winding herself around him like a living vine, opening herself completely to his kiss.

His heartbeat doubled merely thinking about it. God, she'd been sweet. He'd wanted to crawl into her caresses, to drown in the sensations she'd aroused, to bury himself inside her so deep there was no telling where he left off and she began. He'd never before allowed himself to think like that, to fantasize about the shape of her breasts or the feel of her slender legs locked around his hips, and it had been so disconcerting he'd had to stop kissing her. And then he'd started thinking about how she'd grown up practically before his eyes, and then he wondered what Deb would have thought of him kissing Kris…and then he'd been dumb enough to tell her he needed time to figure out their relationship.

He could almost smile about it if he didn't miss her so much. She should have been born a redhead, because it sure didn't take much to set fire to her temper.

He started to punch in her number, then stopped. He'd better decide what he wanted to say, or he was liable to have her jumping down his throat again. *I still don't know what to say to you but I'd like to spend more time with you. I miss you.*

It was that simple. And it was honest. He had a feeling honesty was the only way to go with her.

Decisive now, he did call, and when she answered, he was ready. "Hey, Kris. How are you?"

"Fine." She sounded…cautious. "How about you and Mollie?"

"Mollie's fine." He could talk to her about his day-care problems on the Fourth. "I'm not so fine. I miss you."

She was silent. Finally she said, "I know it's really different now that I'm not around as much. It'll get easier."

It wasn't exactly the response he realized he'd been hoping for. "I don't mean I miss your help with Mollie," he clarified. "I miss *you*. And that's why I'm calling. What time do you want me to pick you up on the Fourth? I thought it might be nice to do the picnic thing again. That was fun last year."

He heard her catch her breath, and she was silent for a moment. "Um, Derek, I can't get together with you and Mollie this year."

Now it was his turn to be silent. "Look, Kris, I'm sorry for upsetting you the other night—"

"No," she said. "It's not that. If I were free I'd be glad to come with you. But I already have a date."

She had a date. A date? He completely forgot what she said about being glad to go along. "With who?"

"No one you know." Her voice sounded pleasant but firm. "He's a new member of the church."

The church that he, Derek, attended on Christmas and Easter while she had taken Mollie to Sunday school all year long. Until recently. "Oh." He wondered if he sounded as shaken as he felt. "Well, maybe we'll see you there."

"Maybe." Her voice was cheery. "Give Mollie a kiss for me."

"I will." What he really wanted was for Kris to give *him* another kiss. But that was looking less and less likely as her words sank in. After another lame exchange of small talk, he hung up—and threw the phone against the wall in a rare display of temper that even he hadn't been prepared for.

"Dammit!" He flopped down on the couch and drummed his fingers on his knees. Alarm bells began to ring in his head. What an ass he was. Here he'd been, thinking nonstop of himself and how a relationship with Kristin would affect him.

It was a shock to realize that she wasn't even thinking of him at all. *If you imagine I'm going to sit home waiting while you dissect your feelings and decide whether or not I might be allowed to fit into your life, you are seriously mistaken.*

God, she hadn't been kidding! He'd disregarded the words, he saw now, because he assumed they were meant to manipulate him. But they hadn't been. His heart sank. No, far from manipulation, Kristin was giving up. Going out with someone else.

The thought made him want to snarl. She had no business going out with another man after she'd kissed him like that! Deb might have been the only other woman he'd ever had a physical relationship with, but he wasn't stupid. He knew he wouldn't lose his head with just any woman like he nearly had with Kris. God, they'd practically spontaneously combusted the other night. He still got hard every time he thought about it.

He was so confused. He wanted her. He didn't want to want her. He was afraid to want her. Kristin was a very different woman than Deb had been. He hadn't ever envisioned himself with anyone besides the wife he'd adored.

Sandy had been right. Kristin was very definitely a woman now. All woman. But she wasn't the woman for him. He should be glad she was dating.

Glad. Ha! He felt anything but. In fact, he felt like throwing a few more things around the room at the thought of Kristin going out with someone else.

Kristin worked late the following Monday. After she checked to be sure the rest of the staff had gone home, she pulled up the computer programs that contained the previous year's daily expense entries. Although it was looking more and more likely that Cathie had been steadily embezzling from the sanctuary, she was still reluctant to believe it. So reluctant, in fact, that she had yet to report it to the board.

As she studied the figures on the screen before her, a note taped to her monitor caught her eye. *Tuesday, 1:00 p.m.*

She'd put it there so she wouldn't forget. Rusty Sheffield had asked her to have lunch with him tomorrow. Although he said he wanted her to catch him up on what she was doing, he'd made it plain that he considered it more than a business lunch. He'd told her how beautiful she'd looked the day of Summerfest. He'd asked her if she was involved with anyone and had made his relief plain when she'd told him no.

It wasn't a lie, she told herself fiercely. *A barely civil friendship with Derek is not a relationship.* And she ignored the little pain that shot through her heart.

She'd promised herself she wasn't going to sit around and moon over Derek. And so she'd said yes to Rusty, and yes to a real date on Friday night with the electrician who'd come by the shelter to repair the wiring. He was young, handsome and single, and she'd be a fool to wait around, hoping Derek would love her someday. This could be her last chance at a relationship!

A knock at the back door of the office startled her, and she quickly minimized the program she had open. Then she went to the door with a pleasant smile fixed firmly in place although the hours posted at the entry clearly stated the sanctuary was closed for the evening. But when she glanced through the window, she recognized Derek's SUV parked beside her little compact car. Her heart rate doubled and her mouth went dry. Good heavens. Had her wishful thinking somehow communicated itself to him?

Ridiculous, she told herself. *You're being ridiculous.* But she couldn't prevent her body's response any more than she could hide the smile that lit her face when she saw Derek and Mollie on the other side of the screen door. *Friendly. Be friendly but not too familiar.*

"What a nice surprise!" she said. "What brings you two my way?"

"I wanted to talk to you," Derek said, "and Mollie wants to see you, too."

Just then, Mollie spotted Hobby, the good-natured retriever mix who was the office mascot. With a squeal, she went racing toward the dog, who obligingly flopped down and exposed his belly for her to rub.

"Well," said Derek wryly, "she *did* want to see you. Looks like you've been upstaged by a dog."

"It wouldn't be the first time that's happened." It was the first time she'd seen him since the night he'd kissed her, and that kiss stood squarely in the middle of her attempt at normalcy. Then she realized she was standing there smiling foolishly. "Come on in. I was still working."

He frowned as he followed her into the inner office, leaning against a file cabinet while she propped herself on the edge of her desk. "This job doesn't pay enough for you to be putting in extra hours."

"I won't once I'm accustomed to everything." She lowered her voice even though she knew no one else was around. "I've been going through the expense entries, trying to find out where that money went."

Understanding crept into his eyes. "And you don't want to do it when anyone's around."

"Right." Her spirits, buoyed by his visit, fell as

she recalled her concerns. "I can't find a thing that points to anyone other than Cathie being the culprit."

"Have you told the board?"

She shook her head. "Not yet."

"You're going to have to tell them soon."

"I know." She sighed. "I just want to check a few more things before I do."

There was a small silence. Derek stuck his head out the door and when he looked back at her, he was grinning. "Mollie's lying on top of the dog."

"Hobby's a patient fellow with children," she said. "How's she doing?"

"Pretty good. Day care is going fine now, thanks to your hair."

She smiled, reaching up a hand to flip a lock forward absently. She'd been wearing it down much of the time since her talk with Faye and she was getting used to the weight of it. "That's good."

"Yeah, except that I'm not going to be able to keep her there."

"What?" She straightened, her voice displaying her concern. "Why not?"

"It's a great place," he said, "but the hours are too confining. I'm going to look for a baby-sitter who can be more flexible when I have to stay late, and who can keep her longer on clinic nights."

"Oh. I never thought about that. Maybe I could—"

But Derek held up a finger. "No. You couldn't. But if you'd be willing to help me interview prospects, I'd be grateful for the additional opinion."

"Of course." He was right. And she should be glad that it had finally sunk into his thick skull that she wasn't going to be Mollie's baby-sitter for the rest of their lives. But…

Another silence fell, this one less comfortable than the one before. Talking about baby-sitting invariably led her to thoughts of the reason Derek needed a sitter, which led to guilt, which in turn made her annoyed with herself because there was absolutely no reason in the world for her to feel guilty for wanting a life of her own.

"So how was your date on the fourth?"

"Fine." If she were honest, it had been a pain in the butt. The man seemed to have more arms than an octopus and all of them had been determined to touch her. She'd never been so glad to get home in her life. She'd practically had to shut the door on him—definitely the best part of the evening.

"Did you enjoy the fireworks?"

"Yes. Did you?"

"Yes, although Mollie missed you. She kept asking when you were coming."

"I'm sorry." And she was. She would much rather have been with Derek and Mollie. But they'd been estranged after that disastrous kiss and she hadn't imagined that he would want her company.

"What did you think of the new rockets they added this year?"

"They were interesting. I like the sounds they make."

"Yeah. We walked around and looked for you, but we didn't see you anywhere."

She stared at him, a suspicion forming in her head as his disconnected statements began to mesh. "Are you trying to find out if I really went to the fireworks?"

To her surprise, a deep flush spread up his neck and he avoided her eyes. "It was kind of odd that we didn't see you."

"Well, I was there." What was going on here? He'd made it plain that he wasn't ready for a relationship, that he wasn't even sure he had liked kissing her enough to want to repeat the experience. He'd said he needed time to figure out what to do about her, as if she were some bothersome task he had to schedule and complete.

"Are you going to see him again?" There was a distinctly challenging note in his voice, one that took her even further aback.

"Why?" Had he always been this tenacious? She was starting to wish she had the nerve to tell him she was sleeping with Craig on a regular basis, but she couldn't bring herself to lie.

"If he's going to be appearing in your life frequently, I want to meet him."

"You know," she said conversationally, holding onto her temper by a thread, "I'm well over the age of consent and you're not my father."

"Are you going to see him again?" He was inflexible. Impossible.

She hesitated, then realized he wasn't going to

back off until she answered him. "Probably not."
She narrowed her eyes. "My dating life is none of
your business."

He shoved off the file cabinet abruptly and headed
out of her office. She followed, completely bewildered and more than a little annoyed, as he bent and
swung Mollie into his arms.

"Give Kristin a kiss," he said to his daughter. And
as Kristin reached out and caught the little girl, Derek
sent her an enigmatic smile over the child's head.
"Everything you do is my business, Kris."

On Thursday night, Faye got fast food for Mollie
and him, although he had to snatch bites of his burger
between patients. By the time he finished examining
the last animal of the evening and got to the fries
they were stone-cold and unappealing, so he pitched
them into the trash. The food was a far cry from the
usual tasty meals he'd enjoyed when Kristin was in
his life.

God, he missed her. He'd stopped by the sanctuary
Monday night hoping to catch her there. But their
encounter had left him dissatisfied and somewhat
alarmed by her evasiveness.

Was she serious about dating other people? He'd
expected to have more time. *More time for what?*

More time to procrastinate, he finally told himself.
More time to tell himself they weren't right for each
other. More time to pretend he wasn't interested,
didn't want her, wasn't going to care if she got in-

volved with some other man. More time to pedal backward every time she came near.

He was, he realized, exactly the same as a woman who said no when she meant yes. He wanted Kristin, he just hadn't wanted to admit it. She'd been right when she accused him of keeping her around for convenience sake, only it wasn't jobs he wanted her for. If she was tied up with him, she was too busy to be going out with anyone else.

Only trouble with that strategy was, she wasn't around anymore. The Fourth of July had been a prime example. As he and Mollie had sat on their solitary blanket at the fireworks, his mind had been a jumble, mixed emotions clouding his brain.

He'd looked for Kris. He'd taken Mollie for a walk through the crowds to buy some caramel corn although his real mission, he could finally allow himself to see, had been to find Kris. But they hadn't seen Kristin and her date, and later, as his daughter dozed off on the blanket beside him and the sky exploded into bright shards of light, all he could think of was Kris. Why hadn't he seen her? It was possible he'd simply missed her, but surely she'd have called out to Mollie, even if she didn't want to talk to him.

Had they decided not to attend? And if not, where were they and what were they doing? He gritted his teeth against the anger that rose once more at the thought of Kristin in another man's arms. He had no right to be mad, he told himself. He wasn't ready to declare himself, wasn't prepared to begin taking her out. He should be glad that she was turning her attentions away from him.

But he wasn't. He felt as if he'd had a bucket of ice water tossed in his face and he recognized that he probably deserved it. *All right,* he told himself. *If you want her, you're going to have to let her know.*

He felt as if he'd been wrapped in insulation since Deb had died, as if his feelings had been cushioned, his interest in the other sex muted by his loss. But now his insulation had been stripped away and all he could think of was how much he wanted Kristin.

Without a conscious decision, he found himself steering the car toward her town house. He was so deep in thought that he was a little startled when Mollie realized where they were and squealed with excitement.

As he climbed out of the car he was suddenly struck by a bolt of uncertainty. Should he be here? Should he be considering altering the friendship he and Kristin had shared for so many years? She'd altered it first, he reminded himself. She'd made him think, made him aware of her, made him *need* again. It was too late to turn back.

He unstrapped Mollie from her car seat and went to Kristin's door. He was just about to ring the bell when he realized the door was open a crack. Cautiously, he poked a finger against it, and when it swung open, he peered into the compact living room beyond.

Kristin lay on the couch, fast asleep.

Good lord. His blood ran cold at the thought of

her lying there, completely defenseless with her front door unlocked to any predator that might come along. Anxiety rose. Was she ill? That wasn't like her, to leave a door ajar.

Setting Mollie down, he crossed the room and knelt at the side of the couch. He cupped her cheek in his palm, relieved to feel the cool silk of her flesh beneath his touch. She wasn't feverish and he felt his inner tension level ease fractionally.

"Kris," he murmured. "Come on, Sleeping Beauty. Time to wake up."

"Tristin?" Mollie squirmed in between his knees and leaned over to put her tiny palm on Kristin's other cheek. "Time to wate up."

Kristin stirred beneath their hands. Her eyelids lazily floated open, and she blinked twice. As she focused on their faces, a luminous smile crossed her face. "I must be dreaming," she said in a soft, husky voice.

She put a hand to Mollie's cheek, but her eyes held his. "Hi."

"Hi! 'Tan I read a 'tory?" Mollie's attention was already diverted.

"Sure. You know where they are." As Mollie wriggled free and dashed off, she continued to stare up at him.

Derek slid his thumb forward and gently brushed it over the full line of her lips, still holding her gaze. "Your door was ajar. I thought something was wrong."

Her eyes clouded. "Heavens. I'm sorry. I'm just

exhausted—I must not have closed it properly.'' As he continued to whisper his thumb over the petal-soft plumpness of her lower lip, she focused on him again. ''Are you sure I'm not dreaming?''

Five

Derek leaned over Kristin. "You're not dreaming." He cast a glance at Mollie, who was already immersed in one of the books Kristin kept in a basket on the floor for her, then looked back at Kristin, his gaze lingering on her lips. They looked soft and warm and he badly wanted to kiss her, to shape and mold and caress until she returned the pressure of his lips.

But not in front of his daughter. "Have you eaten anything?" he asked as he sat back, his hip bumping hers.

She was staring at him as if he'd grown a second head and her eyes were wide and dazed. "Wha—?"

"I'm hungry." He cut her off, not ready to deal

with a discussion of his feelings yet. "If you haven't eaten, we can eat together."

"I haven't," she said absently. "I came home from work and crashed." Then he could see her brain scramble into high gear. "I bet you just finished work and haven't eaten anything, either. Derek, you can't forget to eat. If you get sick you won't—"

He shifted his hand across her mouth, shaking his head. "Do you have any eggs?"

She nodded behind his hand, her gaze locked on his.

"Good," he said. "I'll make us some omelets."

"But—"

"Go get your pajamas on." He stood and headed for the kitchen. "Come on, Mollie. You want to help Daddy cook?"

"Uh-*huh!*" His daughter scrambled to her feet.

He found a skillet, eggs, butter, milk and cheese and with Mollie's "help," started the omelets. He couldn't cook many things but he was competent with the few he could.

By the time he'd set the small table in her kitchen, the first omelet was done and he put it in the oven on a plate to keep it warm until the rest were finished.

Kristin walked into the kitchen a few minutes later, clad in an oversize T-shirt and jogging shorts.

He frowned. "I thought you were going to put your pajamas on."

She rolled her eyes. "These are my pajamas." She fingered the edge of the bottoms. "Minus the shorts."

Minus the shorts. He turned back to the skillet, doing his best not to think about Kristin in nothing but that T-shirt skimming the tops of her thighs. Thighs he could imagine all too well, thanks to those short skirts she'd taken to wearing recently and the trim little shorts that bared a smooth expanse of creamy legs that looked a mile long.

He flipped the last omelet, then withdrew the plate from the oven, slid the omelet atop the others and set it on the trivet he'd placed in the center of the table.

"How about some salad with that?" Kristin retrieved a bag of lettuce and assorted salad ingredients from the refrigerator, added several bottles of dressing and salad bowls, and then they took their seats.

As they always had when they ate together, they clasped hands and let Mollie say the little prayer she'd learned in Sunday school. When Kristin would have withdrawn her hand afterward, he held onto her with a light grip, and she stilled. "I've really missed our meals together," he said quietly. "Thanks for letting us join you."

She sent him an almost shy smile from beneath her lashes. "You're welcome. I'm glad you stopped by."

"Me, too, or your door might have been open all night." He sent her a mock-frown, and when she grinned, he finally began to feel that they were almost back on a normal footing. As normal as it could get, considering.

Derek cut up some egg for Mollie while Kristin dished out salad. It was quiet but comfortable and they listened to Mollie chatter. He allowed Mollie to leave the table after a short while since she already had eaten one dinner and didn't seem terribly hungry.

"Any luck tracing your financial problem?" he asked Kristin. For some reason, he found himself as reluctant as she to give voice to the ugly accusation of embezzlement.

She shook her head. "No, but I have a meeting with Rusty tomorrow at lunch and I'm going to show him what I've found."

"Do you want me to be there?" It was an impulsive offer, born of his concern for her.

Her eyebrows rose and a look of surprise flitted across her features. "I think I can handle it." She smiled at him. "But I appreciate the thought."

He wanted to talk to her about the feelings rolling around inside him, but he wasn't sure how to start. And in any case, he couldn't seem to make himself utter a word.

Kristin's smile faded. She reached over and laid a hand on his arm. "Derek? Are you all right?"

No. How can I be all right when all I can think of is you? And it wasn't just the sexual thoughts that were making him crazy, although they sure weren't helping. He'd always cared about Kristin in a platonic big-brother way. But now there was a more personal element to the way he felt, a tender sweetness that caused his chest to tighten and his heart to pound. It was just friendship, he assured himself. He had cared about her for years.

Aloud, he said, "I'm fine." He laid his free hand over hers where it rested on his forearm. "Will you come over for dinner tomorrow evening? I'm on call, but you know how that goes. It probably will be quiet until about 2:00 a.m.'' He smiled sheepishly. ''And I have an ulterior motive. I'd like your opinion on some of the applications I've received for the nanny position.''

Her smile faded. ''I already have plans for tomorrow evening. I'm sorry. Could we make it Saturday night?''

What plans? Who with? ''Sure,'' he said. He lifted his hand and moved his arm out from under hers, busying himself picking up dishes while he fought the jealousy that urged him to demand she tell him her plans. Was she going out with the Fourth of July date again? Or someone entirely different?

She silently began helping him clear the table, putting things in the dishwasher and setting salad dressings back in the refrigerator. When he risked a glance at her, her expression was unreadable, and an unaccountable streak of annoyance ran through him. He realized he'd expected her to try to smooth things over, to cajole him into talking to her like she always had before when he'd gotten into what she called ''a mood'' about something.

But she hadn't. She acted as if she weren't even aware of his mood, and that made him feel even worse. She'd cared before. He knew she had. But ever since she'd brought up marriage and he'd flipped out, things hadn't been right between them. And now…now he was afraid maybe he'd ruined the relationship he had with her.

She'd said she was glad he'd stopped by. Did she mean that? Was it directed at him, or was she simply pleased that he'd brought Mollie to see her?

No, she'd been smiling at him when she'd said it, smiling in a very feminine way that he was certain had been meant for him.

The telephone rang.

"Oh, rats," Kristin said.

He glanced at her. She'd just plunged her hands into soapy dishwater. "Do you want me to get that?"

She shrugged. "Sure. Thanks."

He reached for the handset in the cradle on the far counter and turned it on. "Hello?"

There was a moment of silence. "May I speak to Kristin, please?" It was a deep, masculine voice.

A wave of sheer, unadulterated jealousy ripped through him. He had to work to keep the satisfaction from his voice as he said, "I'm sorry, she can't come to the phone right now. May I take a message?"

"Sure." The guy sounded ridiculously cheery. "Is this Kristin's father?"

The question caught him flat-footed. Her father? Was the guy kidding? "No," he said, aware that his voice was more than a little testy. "It isn't."

"Oh. Sorry." The man sounded less sure of himself now. "Would you just tell her Rod called to confirm our date tomorrow night? I'll pick her up at seven."

"Sure thing." Derek wanted Rod to come over so he could pound him into the ground.

"Thanks, man."

Derek hung up the handset and slowly turned to Kristin. "That was someone named Rod. He'll pick you up at seven tomorrow night."

"Oh." Her face grew pink. "Thank you," she said in a small voice.

"You're welcome." He clipped out the words, then turned and headed for the living room. "Hey, Miss Mollie, it's time to go home."

"No!" Mollie clutched another book to her breast. "Not done reading!"

"Okay. One more," he said. "You have two minutes to finish that one." He didn't want to have to go back into the kitchen and face Kristin so he leaned against the wall and watched as his daughter became completely engrossed in the pages of the book she was "reading."

"Derek?" Kristin's voice was soft.

He glanced back into the kitchen.

She stood in the middle of the room, one bare foot atop the other, with that glorious out-of-control mane of hair rioting around her and falling over her shoulders. Her hands were absently twisting her T-shirt hem and she'd pulled it so taut that her smooth, flat stomach was exposed. The shirt also outlined the curves of her breasts and he realized she had no idea how she looked to him. How badly he wanted to go to her and smooth a hand down over that delicate skin, to cup her breasts and lower his mouth to them, to see that hair spread over his pillow.

"Are you angry with me?" She was frowning.

"No." *Not exactly.* He didn't move.

"Well, then, what's wrong?"

He shrugged, determined not to give voice to the little green monsters racing around inside him. "I'm just not very satisfied with our relationship right now and I don't know what to do about it." Well, that was honest.

"You don't have to do anything about it." Her chin lifted a fraction.

He turned completely around to face her without saying a word, merely holding her gaze with his until the belligerence drained out of her expression.

He should leave. He was going to leave. He was leaving right now.

He stepped toward her, reaching for her hands, prying her fingers out of the shirt fabric and intertwining his fingers with hers. "I'm not trying to hurt you," he said quietly.

"I know." Her throat moved as she swallowed and suddenly there were tears swimming in her eyes.

"Don't cry," he whispered. "We'll work it out."

"How?" Even though her voice was as quiet as his he recognized the challenge in the single syllable.

A taut, expectant silence hummed between them for a moment.

"I don't know." He felt his shoulders sag. God, what was he supposed to say? Was she still hoping he'd change his mind about marriage?

Without warning, an image of Kristin languidly reclining in his bed, her mane of hair trailing across his white sheets, assailed him. Marriage would give him unrestricted access to her lithe, subtle curves, to her sweet, drugging kisses, to the shattering pleasure he *knew* he could find in her arms.

Marriage. That was crazy. He couldn't marry her. You were supposed to marry someone you loved, not someone for whom you had a critical case of lust overload.

"'Tay, Daddy, I'm ready." Mollie's book banged shut with a loud snap and he heard her scrambling to her feet.

"I'd better take her home." He knew it was a cop-out, saw the ember of hope in Kris's eyes flicker and die. But he was too shaken by his thoughts to figure out what to do or say to repair the damage.

She slipped her hands free from his and walked around him to scoop up Mollie for a tickle and a kiss. "Thanks for making me dinner." But she didn't look at him again. "See you, squirt."

"Bye, Mommy." His daughter threw her arms around Kristin's neck when she knelt and threw herself into Kris's arms so wholeheartedly that Kristin had to put a hand hastily to the floor to keep them both from being pushed right over backward.

Mollie put her hands on either side of Kristin's face and peered deep into her eyes. "Tiss."

"Okay. A nice big kiss and then Daddy will take you home." Kristin suited the words to the action.

Derek opened his mouth to remind Mollie not to call Kristin "Mommy." But then he shut it again without speaking. His throat grew tight and he had to swallow the lump that rose as he watched his little girl hug Kristin. The love in their embrace was undeniable.

Mollie was right. For all practical purposes, Kris *was* her mother, the only one his child had ever known. Kristin had devoted herself to Mollie since her birth, because Deb had been too sick to handle the demands of a healthy infant, and she'd probably spent more time with his daughter than many working mothers did with their own offspring. Already, Mollie had known more of a mother's love than Kristin had in her entire life.

Funny, he'd never really thought of the parallel before. Kristin's mother had died of a cerebral hemorrhage hours after a fall on a patch of ice before Kristin was even a year old. Kris, better than anyone, knew what it was like to be motherless, and she'd devoted herself to making sure Mollie had never felt the same lack.

Was he crazy for refusing to consider a marriage between them?

Kristin rose, taking Mollie's hand. He was prepared for her to avoid eye contact as she had in the past when things had gone wrong between them, so it was a shock to see her smiling at him as she handed off his daughter. An unpleasant shock. The smile was friendly and completely impersonal, as if they'd never kissed, never discussed anything more vital than the weather. And while he was trying to figure out what to say to her in this new mood, she herded them both out her front door. "See you around."

She shut the door and he heard the lock snick into

place before he was even off the stoop. As he strapped Mollie into her car seat, he realized she hadn't said she would see them Saturday night. Was she going to cancel on him?

She met the treasurer of the board of the sanctuary for lunch again on Friday. Rusty was a few minutes late and they ordered immediately, then he sat back and smiled at her.

"So," he said, "I guess you're not keeping Dr. Mahoney's little girl any more now that you're working full-time for us."

She shook her head and smiled. "No." She refused the urge to elaborate and waited for him to speak.

He studied her for a moment, and she wondered what he was thinking. "Kristin," he finally said, "I'll be honest. I'd like to ask you out. I just always thought that you and Derek—"

"—are both very aware that Mollie needs to grow up in a family atmosphere," she finished when he hesitated. "Her mother died just months after she was born, remember?"

He nodded. "Yes. So would you like to—"

"Rusty," she said, "I don't think it would be a good idea for me to go out with someone who's employing me."

"So that means I'd better hurry up and find a permanent executive director, I guess," he said. "Unless I can talk you into accepting the position on a permanent basis. You've stepped in like you've always done the job and I know you'd be an asset to the sanctuary.''

"Not a chance," she said, smiling at him. "I've got plans for myself and they don't include the AAS. Even if it was my father's dream come true."

"Everyone should have the chance to pursue their own dreams." He gave her his most charming smile and not for the first time, she wondered why she couldn't be head-over-heels for someone like Rusty. He was good-looking and athletic and he liked animals. He had his own business that apparently did quite well, judging from the sleek sports car he drove and his membership at the local country club. He had flirted with her since the first time they'd met, but she'd never been interested. She'd never been able to see beyond her feelings for Derek.

Cathie, on the other hand, hadn't liked Rusty at all. He'd asked her out several times when she'd first come to town, but she'd brushed him off consistently. Rusty was a player, she'd always said. And she didn't want a man she'd have to watch for the rest of her life. All she wanted was a good guy who would treat her like precious china and give her children.

"I still can't believe Cathie's gone sometimes," she said.

Rusty sobered immediately. "I can't, either. She was terrific in that position."

"She was a lovely person," Kristin said quietly.

"Well, sure, that goes without saying," Rusty said.

She hated to have to tell him what she'd found but

she had no choice. "Rusty," she said, "I've found a serious problem in the sanctuary's financial statements."

"Oh?" His gaze sharpened. "We're in pretty good shape, thanks to the income from that anonymous trust that came in just before your dad passed away."

"It's not that." Now that she had his attention, she went on to explain about the missing funds.

Rusty looked shocked. "Are you sure?" he asked several times. "Cathie couldn't have done that. Could she?" But there was a kernel of doubt in his tone.

"I can't believe it, either," Kristin said.

"Jeez." He smoothed a hand over his thick, wavy copper hair. "Have you told the police?"

"Not yet."

"So you haven't told anyone else. That's probably a good thing." His tone assumed she hadn't, and she didn't correct him. It hadn't really been a question. Derek was the only other person who knew, and since he was going to be sitting on the board, he would have to know soon anyway.

"I brought a summary of the information along." She handed the folder across the table.

Rusty stashed it in his briefcase as though it might contain illegal drugs. "God, Kristin, be careful with that. The last thing we need is negative publicity for the sanctuary. Can you imagine what would happen to donations if this gets out?"

She shuddered. "I don't even want to think about it. I've been having nightmares already."

"I don't think we should tell anyone yet," he said. "You haven't found anything linking her to this?"

"Not yet," she said.

"Could you possibly be wrong? Could it just be a clerical error with transposed numbers or something?"

She shook her head. "That was the first thing I was hoping for, too."

Rusty sighed and plunged both hands into his hair, resting his elbows on the table. "God, it makes no sense. Why would she have done it? Was she having financial problems?"

"Not that I know of." She shrugged helplessly. She knew how he was feeling. She'd been through all of these thoughts a million times.

"All right." He sighed. "Tell you what. You keep looking to see if there's anything you haven't found yet. I'll make some very discreet inquiries of my banking friends and run a credit check to see if she was spending any odd amounts of money." He shook his head. "There's no point in blackening her good name if she really wasn't involved."

"But who else could it be?" she asked. "You and Walker are the only other two people who could access sanctuary funds, right?"

"Unless," Rusty said slowly, "someone was forging signatures or something."

That hadn't occurred to her and she felt better immediately. Maybe Cathie really hadn't had anything to do with embezzling the money.

She refused dessert on the grounds that she had a

lot of work waiting, and parted company with Rusty soon afterward. As she drove back to the sanctuary, her mind was whirling with thoughts. She'd have to look at some of those cancelled checks again. If it had been done electronically, it would be much more difficult to find.

Kristin's date that evening was fun. Rod, the man she'd met when he came to do some electrical work with the shelter, had told her to dress casually. She was glad she'd heeded his advice and worn a pair of her new denim shorts.

He took her miniature golfing, then to dinner at a Mexican restaurant where they sat outside on a small stone terrace and drank margaritas while their dinners were made. Rod's partner in his business joined them with a date of his own, and although Kristin had never met either of them before, they were pleasant and amusing dinner companions.

He drove a small, modern sports car with a convertible top and he'd folded it down at her request. Rod was unquestionably attractive. He was in great shape, his sense of humor was wicked yet not unkind and his friends were as nice as he was.

And yet she felt a little deflated at the end of the evening when he walked her to her door. She caught herself comparing him to Derek at least five times that evening and she was thoroughly annoyed that she couldn't even go out on a date without thoughts of the wretched man intruding.

Rod, unaware of her mood, slid an arm around her

waist as they walked toward her stoop. At the door, he brought her to a halt, turning to face her. "I had a great time this evening, Kristin."

"So did I," she forced herself to say lightly.

"I'd like to see you again."

"It was fun," she said without committing herself. "I enjoyed meeting Kevin and Leslie."

"How about if I call you next week and we see if we can schedule another get-together?"

"All right." She hadn't actually said she'd go out with him, she told herself. All she'd agreed to was receiving his phone call.

He looked down at her, then put his hands on her shoulders and drew her near. She lifted her face for his kiss, allowing the gentle pressure for a moment before drawing back a fraction, and with a last warm smile, Rod said, "Good night."

"Good night." She waved him off and stood on the stoop for a moment before she turned and unlocked her door. *Rats.* What had she been hoping for? Fireworks? Rod's kiss had been pleasant, but there was no *zing.* At least, not on her part.

She went inside and shut her door, then leaned back against it, thinking. It hadn't left her breathless and shaking, the way she'd felt after that first night Derek had kissed her. It hadn't left her wanting more, wanting to press herself against every hard inch of him, wanting his hands to touch all the secret, throbbing parts of her that quivered with desire.

A knock on the door scared her so badly she actually gave a small scream as she leaped away from the cool surface against which she'd been lingering. One hand flew to the base of her throat. "Who is it?" she called cautiously, pushing the small button that illuminated her watch face. Good grief. It was after eleven. Who in the world—

"It's Derek. Let me in, Kris."

Six

Kristin turned and stared at the closed door. Derek? How could that be? Then she realized that it must be his Friday night on call. He and another local vet took turns covering weekends to give each other a break. But—

"Where's Mollie?" she asked as she pulled the door open.

"Faye's daughter Sissy is keeping her overnight since I'm on call," he said tersely. "Who was that? And didn't you ever learn you shouldn't kiss a guy after a first date?"

She fought back twin surges of jealousy and irritation. Mollie had never had a baby-sitter other than Kristin or Faye before. And what was he doing questioning her?

"You're getting really tiresome," she told him. "How do you know that was our first date? As I know I've said before, I have no intention of telling you about the men in my life." She lifted her chin and started to close the door in his face. "Now if that's all you came by for, I'd like you to leave."

Derek slapped his palm flat against the door, easily preventing her from closing it. "Wait." She heard him inhale a deep breath, then slowly release it. "Kris, just wait a minute." He took a deep breath. "Can I come in?"

She let a tense silence fall while she debated the wisdom of allowing him to enter. But finally, her desire for his company won out over common sense. "All right." She stepped back and opened the door. "But one more question about *anything* that's none of your business, and you're history, buddy."

She hadn't even turned on any lights yet, and the room was barely illuminated by a small crystal lamp whose base she had switched on before she left. She started to move away from him, but Derek caught her hand. "Kris?"

"What?" She avoided looking up at him. Her whole body was tingling with a vivid awareness of how close he was, her breathing coming ridiculously fast, her pulse hammering. Why couldn't she have had this reaction when Rod kissed her? Derek had barely touched her and already he'd gotten more of a physical response from her than poor Rod had the entire evening.

It was a joke, she decided. A great big cosmic

trick, that she would have such intense, serious hots for the one guy who absolutely didn't want her.

Well, perhaps he wanted her, she thought, recalling that heated kiss in his kitchen, but he didn't *want* to, which might be even worse.

Then Derek took her other hand and turned her toward, him, and she forgot about everything else. "I'm sorry," he said, and his voice rang with sincerity. "I didn't come over here to fight with you."

She nodded once. "Apology accepted." She hesitated. "So why *did* you come here tonight? It's not exactly a prime visiting hour."

He smiled, clearly recognizing the conversational olive branch she was extending. "I was called in for an emergency this evening and I just finished. I don't really know why I'm here. I just…came by."

He sounded as baffled as she felt. "All right." She strove for normalcy despite the fact that he was still holding both her hands. "Would you like some iced tea? I made decaf yesterday."

He shook his head. "No tea." His hands tightened as he pulled her closer. "Did you enjoy his kiss?"

She stiffened immediately, averting her face, but he ignored her struggles, folding her against him and holding her there with disgusting ease.

"I hope not." His breath was warm in her ear, his voice a rough velvet rope twining around her and inexorably drawing her closer. "The first time I kissed you, you enjoyed it. So did I. I haven't been able to think about anything but kissing you since then." He cupped her cheek in one big hand and tipped up her chin with his thumb, and his eyes were dark and intense. "I didn't come here for tea or talk, Kris. I came for your kiss."

Dear God. How was she supposed to resist an admission like that? She felt her resistance melt away as if it had never been, and she relaxed against him as he drew her even closer. She grazed the hard line of his jaw with her lips, loving the feel of his haven't-shaved-since-morning stubble. "Then what are you waiting for?" she murmured.

His belly heaved with a silent laugh as he pulled her more securely into his arms and lowered his head. And then his lips found hers, and just like the first time, her whole body exploded into a sizzling, crackling whirl of heat.

This time, she was ready. This time, she lifted herself on tiptoe so that the hard ridge of his arousal fit snugly into the vee where her thighs met, and they both gasped at the exquisite sensation. Lightning exploded through her body, unerringly striking the sensitive flesh between her legs. Without thinking, she twisted against him, increasing the sweet pleasure.

Derek rolled his hips against her and his tongue echoed the thrust as he sought her response. He deepened the kiss, his powerful arms cradling her, one hand sliding down to cup her bottom and pull her even harder against him. She tore her mouth from his, gasping as her head fell back. He barely paused, simply transferred his attention to the slender line of her throat, and she felt his hot mouth tracing a fiery trail down over the slope of her breast. He cupped her breast in one hand and she cried out, arching in his arms as he rubbed a thumb roughly back and forth across her nipple.

And then, with no warning, he froze. His whole big body went rigid against her.

"Derek?"

In response, he lifted his head. One hand still held her clasped against him but the other fumbled at the back pocket of his pants until he'd extracted—

His pager. He peered at the number displayed, and she felt him heave a sigh.

Above her head, he said, "May I use your phone?"

"Sure." Her legs were trembling as she stepped back, but he didn't let go of her hand as he crossed the room, and she nearly stumbled as he towed her behind him.

He picked up the handset and punched in the number with his thumb, then leaned against the doorframe and pulled her to him again.

Bemused, she slipped her arms around his lean waist and put her head on his chest.

"This is Dr. Mahoney," he said into the phone, the deep tones of his voice rumbling in her ear. As he listened, he slowly straightened. "All right. I'll be there in five minutes."

He set down the receiver and she felt him sigh again as he put his arm back around her. He rested his chin atop her head. "I have to go. Dog hit by car."

"Anyone I know?" She strove for a normal tone,

but inside her entire body was quivering with pleasure and happiness.

"Doubt it," he said. "New clients a month ago."
He leaned back and looked down at her, and even in
the dim light she could see his serious expression.
"Tonight changes things."

She regarded him soberly. "Does it?" She'd
thought that after the first time he'd kissed her and
look where that had left her.

"Have lunch with me tomorrow? We can order in
if you like."

"How about I bring lunch?" she offered. "Would
you like me to pick up Mollie or will you have
time?"

His expression changed, a small, private smile slipping over his features, and she felt something low in
her abdomen contract sharply in response. "I'm not
inviting Mollie," he said. "She can join us for dinner
like we planned. It's about time you and I had the
occasional meeting without a pint-size chaperone."

"Oh." It was hard to take a deep breath, and she
hoped he couldn't hear her heart pounding as if she'd
just run a five-minute mile. She was very conscious
of his hard, lean frame pressed against her, and she
wondered why he seemed to be taking this all so in
stride. "All right, then. I'll meet you at the clinic."

"Sounds good." He dipped his head and pressed
one short, hard kiss against her mouth, withdrawing
and releasing her before she could respond. "Noon
tomorrow. See you then."

"See you then," she echoed as he turned and strode to the door.

"Lock it behind me," he instructed before he pulled it shut behind him.

She rolled her eyes fondly as she crossed to the door. Then the full impact of his visit hit her, and her hands began to shake. She locked the door and sank down on the first step of the small landing that led to her second floor.

Had she dreamed what had just happened? Slowly she lifted her hand and touched her fingers to her lips. Derek had kissed her.

Again.

And it hadn't been an impulse that he'd regretted the instant it had ended, either. He'd admitted as much.

A bubble of nervous laughter rolled up and slipped out before she could catch it. Good grief. If one little kiss did this to her...

Only it hadn't been one *little* kiss. It had been several, and anything but small if the solid feel of Derek's body pressed against hers was any indication. Her stomach fluttered as she relived the way he'd ground himself against her, the rasp of his thumb stimulating her nipple.

That page was probably the only reason she wasn't lying naked on her living room rug right this very moment! The thought made her shiver again with helpless anticipation. She'd been practically mindless, responding completely to his touch and taste, overpowered by the reality that exceeded her girlish dreams of making love with Derek. In another minute, she'd have yanked her shirt up and out of the way and offered herself to him.

She dropped her face into her hands and blew out a frustrated breath. Her whole body was humming with arousal. It was a good thing she'd never known exactly how he could make her feel or she might have jumped him months ago.

No. She sobered immediately. Derek hadn't been ready for her months ago. In fact, he hadn't been ready for her a few weeks ago, when she'd first brought up the notion of changing their relationship.

Even tonight, he hadn't sounded sure of his course of action. Even if his body knew exactly what it wanted, Derek was still trying to cope with the sudden shift of reality around him.

She knew it was hard for him to let go of Deb. But she couldn't help hoping. Especially after tonight! She couldn't help thinking that perhaps he soon would be ready to live again.

She'd known and loved Deb, too. They'd spent hours together, as close as the sisters neither of them had ever had. And she was positive that Deb wouldn't have wanted Derek to be alone forever. Maybe it was just rationalizing her feelings, but she believed that Deb would be happy that she loved Derek so much. That she would want them to marry and give Mollie the family she would have had if Deb had lived.

And whether or not he was ready to admit it, he wanted to move on, too. In an about-face that still stole her breath when she thought about it, he'd come to her tonight. He'd admitted he couldn't stop thinking about her. That he wanted to kiss her. That was a huge step forward.

And tomorrow would be another. He'd asked her to come and have lunch with him.

Oh, she'd taken sandwiches by, had actually packed him a lunch, many times in the past. And she and Mollie had run by to visit at lunch countless times as well.

But he hadn't asked her to pack him a lunch, or to bring Mollie. He wanted to see *her*. Just her. She flopped backward onto the landing and kicked her legs into the air in a ridiculous moment of joyous anticipation.

"Hi, everyone." She closed the back door of the veterinary clinic behind her the following day at noon.

She was answered by a chorus of greetings from the receptionists and technicians buzzing around the front desk area.

Sandy glanced up with a smile. "No Mollie?"

"No Mollie," Kristin confirmed.

"Hey, Kristin." Faye waved at her, then pointed toward the hallway. "Derek said to tell you to go on into his office and he'd be in when he could get away. Someone just came by with Chinese takeout." She checked her watch. "He's not running far behind today. Just give him a few minutes." She grinned at

Kristin, then silently lifted her right hand in a fist with the thumb extended upward.

Kristin smiled in return, hoping the rest of the staff hadn't interpreted Faye's meaning, then walked back along the hallway to the door of Derek's office.

The bags of Chinese food were parked on the edge of his desk, so she opened them and began taking the lids off things, tearing open the bags of plastic utensils and laying out the containers of different items.

When the door opened, she spun around. Her heart leaped into her throat and hung there, pounding, while Derek closed the door with a quiet click. "Hi."

"H-hi." She had to clear her throat. "I, ah, I brought several résumés along. The board hasn't advertised the position yet but some of them have invited people they thought might be qualified for the executive director's position to apply. Anyway, they wanted your opinion."

He hung his lab coat on a hook and started across the room. There was a warm, intent expression in his eyes that scattered her thoughts and she felt her pulse began to increase its rhythm.

"My opinion?" As he reached her, he slid his arms around her waist and drew her to him, lowering his head. "My opinion is that if I don't kiss you again soon I'm going to go crazy."

She wasn't ready! Automatically she lifted her arms, palms out in a futile and halfhearted attempt to stop him. It seemed silly, given the way she'd pined for him for so long. But she felt self-conscious and uncomfortable in his arms. They were right here in his office. Anyone could walk in.

Then his lips touched hers and she knew that self-conscious or not, she wasn't going to be able to control her response to him, wasn't going to be able to moderate the need that welled up from deep inside her. Rather than holding him stiffly at arm's length, her hands smoothed up over his shoulders to clasp the back of his neck and slide deep into his hair. She pressed her body urgently against his, shuddering at the feel of his hard, steely frame imprinting itself on her softer one.

His lips were urgent, persuasive, and she opened her mouth helplessly, letting him deepen the kiss in an erotic harbinger of lovemaking. It felt, somehow, as if she'd never really lived before these past few days in his arms. As if she'd been asleep in a walled tower like a fairy-tale princess, waiting for the right kiss to bring her to life.

She was alive now. Oh, she certainly was! Immersed in the wonderful sensation of being touched by the one man in the world who could make her feel so complete, she didn't protest when his fingers slipped beneath the edge of her short blouse. His hand was warm and sure as he traced small circular patterns on her sensitive flesh, his fingers trailing breath-stealing streaks of pleasure wherever they lit. His hand moved up her torso as he kissed her relentlessly, demanding her response as he sought out each rib, slowly exploring her until he was brushing the full undercurve of her breast. He paused there momentarily, lightly brushing his thumb back and forth. Finally, his thumb ventured higher, gently rubbing her stiff and aching nipple through the lacy bra she wore, and her back arched involuntarily as hot, liquid desire shot straight down to the sensitive apex of her thighs.

A small moan escaped her. The sound startled her and interrupted the daze of desire, and she came out of the sensual moment long enough to grab his wrist. "Wait. Someone might come in."

Derek stilled, his mouth and his hand both frozen in place. Finally, he pulled his mouth away from hers, shaking his head as if shaking off a hypnotic spell as he slowly, reluctantly withdrew his hand, caressing her gently as he tugged her blouse back into place. "Whoa. I'm sorry." He blew out a dazed breath as he shook his head. "That got…a little out of hand."

"A little?" Her laugh was shaky as she straightened her shirt.

He stroked a hand down the unruly length of her hair and released her, smiling crookedly. "You sit over there." He backed away from her, waving toward the chair on the other side of the desk. "I don't trust myself when you're within reach."

I don't trust myself when you're within reach. It was true. The muscles of his belly tightened as he looked across the desk at her.

Her hair was a wild, curly tangle and her eyes glowed with warmth. Her lips were red and swollen and there was a pink flush along her jawbone where his beard stubble had abraded her tender skin. He hadn't meant to do that, and he suffered a momentary remorse at marking her. The scariest part was that he couldn't even remember how it had happened.

God! She exploded in his arms, her response a sweet, honest welcome that made it difficult for him to remember his own name, let alone anything else. He'd been celibate by choice in the years since his wife had died and now his body felt as if he were ready to make up for all the thousands of lonely hours in one hot, steamy, endless night.

To distract himself, he said, ''Tell me about these applicants while we eat.''

''All right.'' Kristin pushed a set of utensils at him. He was grateful that she accepted the change of subject so easily. It gave him time to come to grips with the way his world had changed.

A sexual relationship. With Kris. Giving voice to the idea, even if it was only in his head, gave him pause. Was he really thinking of having an affair with her?

He knew how he'd feel if she were contemplating such a course with any other man, and he wasn't sure he even liked *himself* very much for considering her that way. God, this whole situation was making him crazy. Deliberately, he forced himself to set aside his churning thoughts. Kristin didn't appear to be the least bit conflicted as she prepared plates of the Chinese food for each of them. Maybe he was making too big a deal out of the whole thing.

As they ate, she detailed the three individuals who had applied for the executive directorship.

None of them, in his opinion, sounded like what the sanctuary needed. "I'd like to see them hire someone who can take the sanctuary to a new level," he told her. "Someone with experience in fund-raising and marketing. Someone who sees expanding our sights beyond the local efforts in a positive light."

"What do you mean, 'beyond the local efforts'?" She was studying him, her intelligent green eyes assessing as she considered his words.

"State-wide. Nationally, even." He hunted through one of the stacks of literature on his desk, coming up with the magazine he wanted. "This is from a nationally known animal sanctuary in Utah. They get grants, enormous bequests, stuff like that. They have tons of clever programs that encourage people to donate to special projects. And they offer how-to seminars on everything from fund-raising to feral cat colonies." He tapped the magazine with a finger. "You should look at this."

"I will." She took it from him and laid it aside, concentrating on her food. "I've been thinking about the next director, too. I'm going to recommend to the board that they create a contract with a definite end date and a set of goals they'd like to see accomplished in that time. That way, they'll be able to measure how well someone is working out and give themselves a way to release an employee who isn't living up to expectations. If we were to hire someone like you're talking about, that would be a vital part of the contract.''

His eyebrows rose. "Great idea." He cleared his throat, remembering a conversation he'd had with Rusty a few days before. "Have you considered staying in the position?"

She cocked her head. "Permanently?"

He nodded. "Rusty mentioned to me that the board wanted to ask you to accept the job for good."

"He hinted at it." She shook her head. "Not interested. Although I'm enjoying the challenge, I still want to keep my accounting practice. I'm actually planning on expanding it once you find the right person for the executive director's job."

"Expanding it?" He had never really spoken much with Kris about her work, he realized with a pang of guilt. Most of the time, they talked about Mollie or about things that went on in his practice, about the upkeep of his home or about the sanctuary. He couldn't remember the last time it had occurred to him to ask her about her goals and dreams.

She nodded. "I can go full-time. It would be a nice leap in my income level, let me finally get out from under—oh, never mind. I'm sure this is boring you to tears." Her gaze slid away from his and she concentrated on her food. "Tell me how Mollie is doing. Are you still planning on looking for another private sitter?"

Derek studied her in silence. What the heck had just happened? She'd been discussing her business when suddenly she'd stopped making eye contact, her posture had changed from relaxed and easy to straight-backed and rigid, and she'd fixed on a bright, fake smile that he didn't think he'd ever seen before. "Yeah," he finally said. "I still need a sitter. But Mollie's enjoyed day care so much I'm thinking of signing her up for preschool a couple of days a week. It'll be part of the sitter's job to take her and pick her up."

The odd smile faded from Kristin's face and a genuine, far more familiar frown replaced it. "You mean you're going to let a total stranger drive her around?"

"Well, yeah." Although he hadn't really even considered that aspect of the idea.

"What if the person has an old rattletrap of a car? How will you know if he or she has a safe driving record? What will you do about a car seat—?"

"Hold on!" He held up one hand, palm out. "This is just something I was considering. I haven't interviewed anyone yet, and I honestly hadn't even thought about car safety. Do you want to help me put together a list of questions?"

She nodded immediately. "Sure. And as long as I'm making suggestions, why don't you see if there are any agencies in the area that provide nannies? We'd still want to conduct our own interviews and check references, but at least we'd know they'd come recommended with some initial screening done."

We. Two little letters that made one very simple word. But something in the way she said it struck him like a bolt of lightning from a cloudless sky. *We*. When had it begun to sound so good to him?

He finished his meal, then came around the desk and held out his hand to her.

She looked at his outstretched hand, then up at his face. Slowly, she placed her palm in his and let him draw her to her feet.

Neither of them said a word. Still holding her gaze, he drew her into his arms and lowered his head. The moment his lips touched hers, he felt the same thrill as he had before. The irresistible call of desire, of need and passion and heat and all the things he'd missed for so long and had found in her arms. He kissed her deeply, plunging his tongue into her mouth in search of her uniquely exciting response, delighting in her slick, soft flavor. His hands slid down her back, stopping just above the sweet swell of her bottom. His palms practically itched with the need to slide farther down and cup the soft globes, but this wasn't the place to grope her like an adolescent boy. The last thing he wanted to do was make her uncomfortable. Besides, if he started, he wasn't at all sure he'd be able to stop. So much for noble motives.

He reached up and tugged lightly on her arms, drawing them down from his neck and holding them between their bodies. ''Much as I'd like to do this for the rest of the day, I've got to get back to work.''

Kristin's eyes were soft and dazed, her lips red and full. She blew out a breath as her forehead dropped to rest against his chest. ''It's probably just as well,'' she muttered.

He found he didn't like the sound of that sentiment. ''Why?''

She looked up at him, her tone mildly exasperated. "Derek, it hardly seems fair for me to be kissing you like this. You know I'm dating several men right now and I'm certainly not carrying on with them like I just did with you."

I'm dating several men. A primal surge of jealousy and possessiveness rushed through him. "You'd better not be." His voice sounded thick and rough to his own ears, and he didn't wait for her to respond before he bent his head and took her mouth again. He released her wrists and took her by the hips, tugging her firmly against his body, knowing she couldn't miss the pulsing column of arousal that hadn't completely subsided since he'd walked into the room. The hell with not making her uncomfortable. She could damn well feel as uncomfortable as he did right now.

"No more dating," he said, lifting his mouth a breath from hers. "I told you the other night that things have changed."

"But—"

"This is going to be an exclusive relationship," he told her.

"Exclusive in what way?"

God, did the woman have to argue with every word that came out of his mouth? "Neither of us is going to see anyone else from now on."

She frowned. "You weren't seeing anyone before. I'm the only one who's concerned about my life passing me by." Her eyes looked suspiciously moist. "I can't just be your sexual toy, Derek."

He rubbed his hands up and down over the slender line of her back, feeling the delicate bone structure beneath his palms. Despite her youth, Kristin was one of the most capable, competent women he'd ever known. He thought of her as self-assured, as sturdy and indestructible.

Perhaps too much so. He'd ignored her need for reassurance, for support and commitment because it hadn't occurred to him that she needed those things. Now he knew she did. She was as vulnerable, in her way, as any other woman.

A fatalistic sense of calm descended, and he knew what he was going to say mere moments before he opened his mouth. "I don't want you to be a sexual toy. I want you to be my wife."

Seven

The words were shocking, even to him. Derek suddenly couldn't draw a deep enough breath and an instant tension stiffened his limbs.

Kristin froze in his embrace. She didn't say a word.

"Kris." He stepped back and took both her hands in his, then took a deep breath and dropped to one knee in front of her. "Will you marry me?"

God. The sound of the words hitting the air was nearly a physical pain in his heart. He'd spoken those words once before, holding Deb in his arms on a park bench just as a brilliant sunset feathered across the sky.

He and she had been young. So young. Who could

have known that she'd be dead in just over a decade, years before her time?

Kristin was still standing in front of him, and he forced himself to set aside the painful thoughts. The past was over. Buried.

And he realized she hadn't said a word.

He cleared his throat and tried to smile. "I, ah, didn't think you'd find a marriage proposal from me abhorrent."

"It's not that," she said slowly, soberly. "It's shock. You didn't want to marry me last month. What's changed?"

"I didn't know what I wanted last month. Not even last week," he said honestly, trying to give her question the respect it deserved. "Ever since you first brought up the idea of marriage my head's been in a spin. I thought I was content with the way my life was going, but I don't think it was contentment I was really feeling. I was in a rut and it was easier to stay there than to look for a new path."

Kristin swallowed. Her eyes were wide, a dark mossy green filled with shock. "And the new path is asking me to marry you?"

He rose and smiled down at her. "It's not a new path, is it? It's one that I've been avoiding taking for too long now."

Something moved in Kristin's eyes, some screen dropped and he was momentarily seared by...by what? What had he seen? Pain? Anger? "Wow," she said. "Overwhelm me with romance, Derek."

Romance. The word reminded him of Deb again,

of the excitement and anticipation he'd felt during their courtship and early years together and a wave of grief stronger than he'd felt in months swamped him. This was nothing like that. And he didn't want her thinking, *couldn't* have her thinking or hoping it could be. A lump rose in his throat and he had to pause for a moment before he could speak.

"Look," he said. "I'm not young and romantic, Kris. What we have between us isn't romance, but it's just as good in many ways. Friendship, dependability, shared interests." He lowered his voice. "I can promise you that I'll be faithful. And I think we've safely established that we've got chemistry on our side."

"Sexual compatibility is nice, but it's certainly not a good reason to marry someone," she pointed out.

He was beginning to feel a little frazzled. What the hell did she want from him? Hadn't he just done exactly what she'd wanted? "I'll be a good provider. You can work or not, I don't care, as long as we have good child-care arrangements for Mollie."

"And other children?" Her voice was little more than a whisper, but the question froze him in place.

More children? God, he'd never even considered that possibility. He'd been stupid not to, he saw now. Kristin was a young woman. Of course she would want children of her own.

Children of her own. Children with him. It was almost hard to breathe in the close confines of the little room. "I, ah, I need some time to think about that," he managed to say in what he hoped was a relatively normal tone. "I see that we have a lot more issues to think through than I'd first considered. Let's talk more tonight."

"You still want me to come over for dinner?" She sounded vaguely surprised and he realized he hadn't been all that successful at concealing his turbulent emotions from her after all.

"Yeah." He put out a hand and stroked the back of his fingers down her cheek. "I do. Will you come?"

She smiled, although he thought it seemed a little shaky. "All right."

It took all the nerve she possessed to force herself to approach the front door of her childhood home at seven that evening. She'd been letting herself in with a key for years, first when it was her home and more recently after Deb's death. But tonight Kristin felt like a stranger as she stood on the stone front porch holding a plate of the rice cereal treats that she knew both Mollie and Derek loved.

She rang the doorbell and shifted restlessly from foot to foot as she heard Mollie's racing footsteps. Derek's heavier tread approached at a more sedate pace. She was afraid when she opened her mouth to speak all the butterflies in her stomach were going to spill right out in a wild, bright-colored swarm and flit away. Of course, they would have left behind co-coons chock-full of new ones to replace them.

The door swung open and even though she was expecting it, her stomach lurched. Derek stood facing her as Mollie danced madly in front of him, chattering a welcome. Over the little girl's head, their eyes met and the breath whooshed out of her lungs at the heated awareness in his blue gaze. Her abdomen contracted sharply as he surveyed her from head to toes and back again. She'd taken special care with her appearance tonight, not wanting to be too dressed up and yet wanting to be sure he noticed her.

From the look in his eye as he checked out her sleeveless, scoop-necked aqua sweater and short, beige linen skirt, she'd succeeded. "Hi," he said.

"Hi." She didn't know what to say to him; the things they needed to talk about weren't issues that could be easily discussed with the distraction of a child.

Mollie grabbed her hand and tugged her into the foyer. "Come see my new baby Daddy bringed!"

"A new baby?" Feeling unbelievably skittish and shy, she concentrated on Mollie. "What's her name?"

"Zu-zie." The little girl took her hand and tugged her toward the family room.

"Ah. Susie. I like that name," Kristen said. She glanced over her shoulder at Derek and caught him grinning.

"Shall I take those?" he asked, indicating the dessert bars.

"Yes, please," she said. "But don't you dare eat any before dinner." And with that small exchange, she suddenly felt much more comfortable, as if the world had righted itself to a more familiar perspective.

Derek snapped his fingers. "You know me too well."

"And don't you forget it." She returned his smile and their eyes held for a long moment. But it didn't make her nervous or jittery this time. It was true. She did know him well. She couldn't think of a single thing she could be asked about him that she wouldn't know.

Mollie claimed her attention again then, and while Derek got dinner on the table, she played with the little girl. As she did so, she realized how much she had missed these times together. Mollie seemed to have grown taller just in the short time since Derek had enrolled her in day care. And she was learning to tie "bunny ears," she informed Kristin. A pang of loss shot through her heart at that news.

And then a different feeling smote her heart. If Derek really wanted to marry her, Mollie would be *her* daughter, just as she'd imagined so many times in her daydreams. It was almost too much to hope for, and she forced herself to turn off the frantic thoughts vying for notice in her mind.

She read the little girl several stories. After that, while Mollie became engrossed in folding her baby's blanket, Kristin got up and moved into the kitchen. She felt odd, acting like a guest when she knew how hectic Derek's life was. He didn't need the added stress of entertaining.

"Need any help?" she asked him, automatically opening the drawer where the flatware was kept.

He smiled, but shook his head. "Believe it or not, I have everything under control. I set the table earlier so I wouldn't have to worry about it, and the potatoes should be just about done. Why don't you just sit down over there and keep me company?"

"Nobody needs me anymore, just as I predicted," she said, trying for a light tone as she perched on one of the bar stools at the center island. "Mollie's learning to tie and you're managing to cook."

"Hold on a minute." Derek set down the spoon he'd used to stir the green beans and came around the corner of the island. "We may be learning a few new tricks but we'll *always* need you, Kris." He reached for her, pulling her into his arms, and she instantly felt the lack of oxygen to her brain at the feel of his hard, warm body against hers. She hadn't expected the embrace, hadn't expected him to act like a lover, although that made little sense given the way he'd acted earlier in the day. Still…she'd been in and out of his home for years as a friend and the sudden shift felt distinctly weird.

He kissed her lightly, but before she could respond he released her and walked back to the stovetop. "I'd better get this meal on the table."

It was wonderful to sit down and have a meal with Derek and Mollie again, and afterward she convinced him to let her give Mollie her bath while he cleaned up the kitchen.

"I meant for you to be strictly a guest tonight,"

he told her ruefully as Mollie raced ahead of her up the steps.

"Derek, I *want* to do this," she said. "I've missed you two terribly."

"Exactly what 'this' have you missed, Kris?" he asked, his brows drawing together. "You're the one who quit coming around, who quit eating with us."

"Who quit cleaning your house and helping with your laundry." She could feel her temper rising at the censure in his tone.

"Don't put words in my mouth. It wasn't what you did that we missed, it was your presence."

She didn't know what to say to that. So in the end, she said nothing. But as she turned and started up the stairs, Derek said quietly, "Once Mollie is in bed, you and I are going to finish this conversation."

Derek paced around the family room, too nervous to sit. Kris was still upstairs reading Mollie one last story after he'd said good-night, but she couldn't linger much longer.

He was impatient, which was rare in itself. Normally he was content to allow the passage of the days, to let events and incidents come about in their own good time. He also, he admitted, was a master at ignoring anything he didn't want to face. That was the only reason why he'd allowed himself, Mollie and Kris to drift along like this for so long.

Kristin was right. They had to move on, one way or another. And the one way he couldn't countenance was not to have her in his life.

He took a deep breath, blew it out. The more he thought about it, the more a marriage between them made sense. He wanted it. Wanted her. But not just for the sex, although he was still stunned at how hot and wild the passion between them could flare—

"You look as nervous as I feel."

He spun around and there she stood in the doorway. The aqua sweater set off her fair skin and made her eyes look even greener by contrast. It hugged her curves and the short skirt showed off her shapely legs, reminding him of how effectively she'd hidden herself from the world for so long.

"Why did you do that?" he asked before he could stop himself.

"Do what?" She looked puzzled as she walked forward and took the seat he indicated on the couch.

He made a general up-and-down motion that encompassed her figure. "You used to wear baggy shirts and jeans all the time. Now you look…you look like a woman."

Her face crinkled into amusement but a pretty blush crept into her cheeks as she laughed aloud. "If that was a compliment, thanks."

He felt his face heat as well, but he said calmly, "Oh, it was. Let me rephrase that. Now you have curves that drive a man wild just thinking about what you look like beneath your clothes. That drive *me* wild," he amended, looking her straight in the eye.

She looked away first. "Wow." She blew out a breath. "I can't get used to talking like this with you."

He used the opportunity to lower himself beside her, stretching out his long legs, slipping out of his shoes and crossing his ankles with his heels propped atop the solid coffee table before them. Kristin was sitting bolt upright beside him as he slouched down onto his spine, and he took her by the elbow and tugged her backward, sliding his arm around her at the same time. Smooth, if he did say so himself.

She allowed him to draw her close but he could tell she was still stiff and ill at ease, so he picked up the remote off the arm of the couch. "Want to catch the news?"

They sat in silence for a long while, absorbing the top stories of the day. It was largely depressing stuff, focused on political maneuverings, war and civil upheaval around the globe, spectacular fatalities and grim reports of worldwide illness and famine. After a while, Kristin sighed. "I'm probably crazy to be considering bringing more children into this world, aren't I?"

The atmosphere in the room changed instantly but he forced himself to stay relaxed. She didn't look at him, but kept her gaze directed at the television, so he followed suit. "Deb and I talked a lot about that, before we decided to have children," he said. "But I think seeing the news like this gives you an inflated feeling of pessimism. There's a lot of good in the world as well. It just doesn't make for great ratings like the bad stuff does."

Out of the corner of his eye, he saw her smile. "Well put. And probably true."

He took a deep breath. "So…you want children?"

She turned her head and looked straight at him. "I want *your* children." There was a small, electric silence, and she hurried on. "I'd like Mollie to have at least one sibling. I was an only child and always envied kids with brothers and sisters. They seemed more like a real family to me."

I want your children. All he could seem to think about was how they were going to create those children, and he felt his body stirring and responding to the images he couldn't shove out of his brain. Then he realized she was still speaking.

"…thought any more about whether or not you want more kids?"

"Yeah," he said. "I mean, I have, and I think you're right. Mollie should have siblings. And honestly, I don't just want more children because of Mollie. I like being a father. I always imagined we'd have several…" He let the sentence trail off, realizing that it probably wasn't such a great idea to talk about his first wife to the one he hoped to marry next, even if it was Kristin, who'd known and loved her, too.

"I think that would please Deb," Kristin said steadily. "She always wanted a small tribe, remember?"

Relief rushed through him. Kristin understood him, understood what he was thinking. She always did and he shouldn't forget that. "So," he said, tightening his arm a little. "We've agreed that we both want more children. And I've told you how I feel. I don't only want you because of Mollie, although knowing how much you care for her is a great part of the package. So what do you think?'' He turned his body slightly to face her a little more fully. "Will you marry me?''

A small smile curved the corners of her mouth as he looked down at her. "Yes.''

Relief poured through him. He put his free hand up to her cheek and cradled her face. "You won't regret it,'' he told her, skimming his thumb along the line of her jaw. "We're going to make a good team.''

Her smile widened. "We already do.''

He kept looking down at her, wondering why in the world it had taken him so long to see how lovely she was. "How soon do you want to get married?''

She shrugged. "I don't know. Soon?''

"How about next Sunday?''

Her emerald eyes widened. "As in one week and one day away?''

He nodded.

"Derek, we can't possibly plan a wedding in such a short time!''

"I don't know that we have all that much to plan,'' he said carefully. He should have realized that Kristin would be thinking in terms of a *real* wedding, with guests and flowers and cake and all the attendant hoopla. "I'd like to have a simple ceremony,'' he said, "and unless it's really important to you, I'd rather forget a reception and all that jazz. I can't take a honeymoon right away but if I start arranging it now, I should be able to get away in a couple of months.'' He and Deb had had a huge wedding with scads of family and friends, a ridiculous number of attendants, and a dance band at the lavish reception. There was no way he could go through anything like that. It would remind him too much of…of the way his life was supposed to have been.

Suddenly, he realized Kristin hadn't said a word in response yet. Hell. Had he completely screwed this up?

But then, as he was frantically trying to figure out how to explain his feelings to her, she nodded once, briskly, and said, "That's fine."

"It is?" He couldn't keep the surprise from his tone, but he covered it quickly. "Okay. That's settled, then. All we have to do is get blood work done and apply for the license." He shifted, pulling her across his lap as he tried to cover the awkward moment just past. "I don't want to wait, Kris. I want you in my home."

"I don't want to wait, either," she told him. She put her arms around his neck as her words echoed between them. He knew she'd been talking about marriage, but he could see from the sudden awareness in her eyes that she had caught her unintentional double entendre just as he had.

Slowly, holding her gaze with his, he pulled one of her hands from his neck and laid his lips against the fragile skin of her inner wrist. Using his tongue, he tested and tasted his way up her arm, lingering at the tender fold of her elbow, then sliding his lips farther up to her shoulder before skimming across the thin strap of the aqua sweater and laying his mouth on her collarbone.

Kristin's head fell back and her eyes closed as her body slackened in his arms. Her hands moved to clasp his shoulders as he nibbled her neck and pressed light kisses up the line of her jaw until his mouth hovered over hers. "Kiss me, Kris," he breathed.

He shifted his supporting arm higher to bring her head up, delighting in the willing way she lifted her mouth to his. Her lips were soft and sweet and he leisurely explored their shape for long moments before flicking his tongue across the seam of her lips. When she opened her mouth, he moved inside immediately, his tongue tangling with hers in hot, slick pleasure. As they kissed, her lithe body twisted in his arms, pressing against the growing arousal that pushed at his pants, making him all too aware that it would only take a few smooth moves to have his pants unzipped and her astride his lap.

He shuddered. "I probably shouldn't be doing this," he said. But he couldn't resist sliding one hand over the enticing swell of her hip. He smoothed a path down her upper leg to where the short skirt stopped and uttered a silent alleluia at the feel of her soft bare thigh beneath his palm.

She placed her hands flat against his chest, palms side by side. "You can," she whispered, "if you want to."

"Oh, I want to," he said, hearing his own voice come out a deep, rough growl, "but I don't want to rush you. We can wait until we're married.'' A small, ignoble part of him sat up and shouted *No, no, no!* but he disregarded it. He was telling the truth; he *didn't* want her to regret anything about their first time together. Still, it was all he could do to prevent himself from twisting his torso back and forth beneath the warm pressure of her small hands.

''You're not rushing me,'' she said obliquely. She wouldn't meet his eyes but kept them fixed on her hands. A surprising tenderness surged through him as he realized she was feeling shy. She was shy!

Of all the things he associated with self-possessed, confident Kristin Gordon, shy probably wasn't anywhere near the top of the list. And yet…she was looking to him to take the lead.

Another realization swept over him. Kristin might be self-assured and smart as a whip about most things, but in this arena, he was definitely the more experienced of the two of them. Experienced…experience. Carefully, not wanting to spoil the moment, he said, ''Kris? I, ah, don't quite know how to ask you this, but—''

''I'm not a virgin.'' Her voice was still soft, her eyes still averted.

He couldn't define the emotions that rushed through him at that one small sentence. Relief, maybe a little. He and Deb had both been virgins their first time together and it hadn't been a stellar experience for either of them. He'd been fast; she'd been slow. He knew he'd hurt her, but had been so overwhelmed by basic adolescent lust that he'd had no hope of making it good for her, and he'd felt terribly guilty.

Another emotion overshadowed his momentary recall. It seemed almost like…like jealousy. He tried to tell himself it was fatherly outrage, but that didn't wash.

"Who?" he managed. "When…?" The thought of some other man touching her intimately made him see red.

"It was a long time ago," she said softly. "My second year in college. And not something I was inspired to repeat."

Tenderness swept through him, washing all other feelings away. "Let me inspire you then," he said. He lifted her from his lap and stood, then bent and swung her into his arms. She was easy to carry, although she struggled wildly for a moment before clutching him around the neck. "Derek! What are you doing?"

"Taking you to bed," he told her, striding from the room. "We're going to do this right."

Eight

Had she known all along that this was how the evening would end? Had her subconscious picked up on something she hadn't noticed? Was that the reason for the extraordinary case of nerves she'd been feeling?

As Derek carried her up the stairs and shouldered open the door to his bedroom at the far end of the hall from Mollie's, Kristin decided to stop thinking, stop analyzing and simply enjoy. She'd imagined making love with Derek so many times but her dearth of experience had limited the scope of her dreams to the basics. Tonight, she wouldn't have to dream anymore.

It was fast. Probably too fast, in the context of a normal dating relationship. She would no more think about sleeping with a guy on the first date than she would about flying to the moon. And under no circumstances would she sleep with a man while his child was in a room just down the hall.

But this wasn't a normal dating relationship. In actual fact, they'd never even had a real date. Instead, they'd lived in each other's pockets for years, sharing the joys and worries of raising a baby girl. They'd spent hours discussing his business and the sanctuary, had made snowmen together and sung "Eensy, Weensy Spider" until they were both ready to scream. They'd shored up each other through times of grief, celebrated birthdays and shared silly jokes over a sinkful of dirty dishes.

No, it couldn't be further from a normal dating relationship. But it wasn't fast in any but the most literal sense of the word, either. She knew him better than she'd ever known any man besides her father. She trusted him with her body in a way she could never trust anyone she'd only known weeks or months.

They belonged together. And in just a short time, they would be married. Married! She still couldn't quite believe it. But as Derek carried her into his bedroom and gently laid her on his bed, it became real in the most basic sense of the word. He switched on a small lamp that cast a dim glow over the room before he came down beside her and she had no more time for thought as he covered her mouth with his, kissing her with urgent demand. One of his legs slid over hers, pinning her in place, and she could feel his body surging against her hip as his breathing grew short and choppy. She put her hands to his neck and then slipped them up into his hair, kneading his scalp and holding him fast to her while his lips left hers and moved down her neck. He had one arm beneath her. The other lay heavily on her stomach, and she felt the muscles of her abdomen contract sharply when he spread his big hand wide, his little finger stretching down almost to the top of her feminine mound. A sudden surge of excitement danced through her and she rolled her hips up involuntarily, moving his finger over her. Her body was throbbing deep between her legs, aching for his touch and her breast heaved with frustration.

Derek chuckled deep in his throat. "Not so fast. I've been having fantasies about this for days. I don't want to rush."

Slowly, he slipped his hand up her torso until he had covered her breast. He didn't move, just held his hand there, cradling her gently. "You had me fooled," he told her, lifting her head to look into her eyes. "I didn't have any idea how beautiful your body was. I feel like a man coming out of a coma and just noticing the world around him for the first time."

She smiled, raising her torso just the smallest bit, pressing herself more firmly into his palm. "I had most people fooled, I guess."

"Why?" he asked. "You never answered me earlier."

She shrugged, and the motion moved her breast

beneath his hand, sending ribbons of pleasure snaking through her. "I never cared much what I looked like before. But when you said no to my proposition—"

"Your proposal," he corrected her.

"I realized that if I wanted to find a man I was going to have to learn how to attract one."

He frowned and his eyes darkened. "So you started wearing revealing clothes, thinking that was the way to get noticed?"

"It worked on you," she said, refusing to let him draw her into an argument. "So don't be hypocritical." She ran her hands down to his shoulders and over the heavy muscle of his upper arms, her fingers lingering to stroke and caress. "Can we talk later?"

He relaxed, a fleeting smile touching his mouth. "Yeah. We can." He rose to his knees beside her. "Right now, I think you need to get out of these clothes."

His hands were gentle as he tugged the aqua sweater over her head. She heard him suck in a harsh breath as his eyes blazed down at her breasts, and she thanked heaven that tonight she'd had the sense to wear the new sheer black lace bra and panty set she'd just bought. He placed both his hands over her breasts, cupping the full mounds and she shivered at the passion blazing in his blue eyes.

"You, too," she said, although it came out as little more than a husky whisper.

"Help me." He lifted her to her knees beside him on the mattress and set her hands at the top of his shirt placket. Her fingers were actually trembling as she unbuttoned each button. As she approached his belt buckle, he pulled the remaining fabric of his shirt out of his pants so she could continue. When all the buttons had been slipped free of their moorings, she slowly spread the shirt wide, sliding her palms up his chest and out over his shoulders until the shirt fell down past his elbows and he was able to shrug out of the rest of it.

His chest was broad and solid, dusted with a faint ''T'' of dark hair that arrowed down to his navel and disappeared beneath the waistband of his jeans. He reached up to his shoulders and captured her hands again, drawing them down between them and she realized he wanted her to unbuckle his belt as well. She swallowed.

The one time she'd had sex in college, it had been dark and furtive, and the guy had left practically as soon as he'd finished. She'd never seen a naked man's body in her entire life.

And while she understood that he was allowing her to get comfortable with her own state of undress, she couldn't seem to make her fingers move. She glanced up at him, and he smiled as he lowered his head and took her mouth again, pulling her to him and kissing her thoroughly until the fire inside her was raging again and she was twisting against his hot, bare chest, wanting, needing more contact.

She felt his fingers at her back for a moment, and then he was tugging her bra down her arms, tossing it aside. He made a single rough, hoarse sound and the room spun for a moment as he laid her back on the bed again. His hands were swift and sure, taking her skirt and panties off in a single motion, and when she was naked, he hovered over her for a long moment, his eyes traveling over every inch of female flesh he'd revealed. He lifted a hand and laid it gently right over the triangle of crisp, curling hair, and one corner of his mouth kicked up. "A natural blonde," he said softly. And then he was gone, moving off the bed to get rid of the rest of his own clothing.

Kristin lay watching as he stepped out of his pants. He wore stretchy, snug briefs that did nothing to hide the ridge of arousal beneath and her pulse raced. He was barely contained by the fabric, and in a moment he hooked his thumbs in the sides of the briefs and shucked them off as well. She couldn't look away, couldn't pretend to be matter-of-fact. He was big, heavily made and if a man could get any more aroused, she couldn't imagine how. He slowly put one knee on the bed again, and as he leaned forward, his sex fell against her belly and she jumped. He was hot and hard, so hard, and without conscious thought she wriggled her hips beneath him, seeking a satisfaction that eluded her.

Derek lowered himself slowly onto her, pushing her thighs apart and making a space for himself. The action sandwiched him between their bodies and she could feel him, firm and gently moving against her belly. He bent his head to her breast then, and she jumped as his lips closed over one nipple. He swirled his tongue around the tight peak time after time, and just when she thought she couldn't stand the rising tension any longer, he drew her deeper into his mouth and began to suck strongly at her. She almost shrieked aloud, her body surging up against him as electric shocks of sensation ran straight from her breast to her womb. She was trembling, panting, her legs moving restlessly around his hips.

Derek made a low sound of approval. He shifted to one side and she opened her mouth to protest his leaving, but the words turned into a breathless moan of pleasure as his fingers slid up the inside of her thigh. He brushed lightly over the curls he found there and she was startled to realize how wet she felt. Then one finger probed deeper, sliding between her soft folds and her back arched as he suddenly pushed the digit deep, deep inside her sensitive channel. There was no pain, only an exciting sense of pressure and an irresistible urge to move against his hand. He laid the fleshy pad just below his thumb flat against her and pressed strongly, and she clutched at his shoulders. "Derek, I want...Derek!" His name became a cry of release as the tight coil of desire that had drawn together inside her suddenly flew apart. Her body was out of her control, bucking and surging against his hand, her back arching repeatedly as her fingers gripped his shoulders. He touched her relentlessly, pushing her beyond pleasure into a final paroxysm of climax that left her limp and gasping, too drained to move, completely shocked by the force and power of her first orgasm.

Then, before she could recover, before she had

time to get embarrassed at her own abandon, he drew
his hand away and levered himself over her again.
She could feel the heavy length of him as he drew
back on his knees and placed himself directly at the
moist, pouting entrance to her body. Slowly, he
flexed his hips, using his hands to open her to him,
and she shivered at the first blunt, probing contact.
He leaned forward, supporting himself on his arms
as he pushed himself deeper.

"Kris."

She looked up at him and was startled by the
fierce, intent look on his face.

"Put your legs around my waist," he commanded.

She obeyed instantly, wrapping her arms around
his broad shoulders and linking her ankles behind his
lean waist. The position tipped her up into an even
more intimate contact and she drew in a sharp breath.

He grinned, a mere baring of his teeth, and muttered, "Hang on," and almost before the words reg-
istered, he was moving strongly against her, gasping
as his body arched against her in the throes of his
own fulfillment.

When he finally was still, he lifted himself away
from her and rolled to one side. He pulled her against
him, kissing her temple gently as she cuddled close.
"You all right?"

She couldn't suppress a smile. "I'm fantastic."

Now it was his turn to grin. "Yeah. You are."

They stared at each other a moment as the smiles
faded, and she wondered at the searching look in his

gaze. Finally, he said, "Thank you for being persistent. And patient."

"You're welcome," she said, equally seriously. Her heart was beating faster at the tender expression on his face.

"Spoons?" he asked.

She was completely bewildered. "Spoons? What does that mean?"

"Do you want to sleep spoons?" He turned her to her side and curved his body around hers, pressing her back against his chest and her bottom into the cradle of his hips. Sliding one arm beneath her, he said, "Isn't this nice?"

"Yes." Her voice was a whisper. "Very nice." In all her imaginings, she'd never pictured herself sleeping with him in such an intimate, loverlike embrace. It was more wonderful than her best dreams. Twisting her head backward, she stretched up and kissed his jaw. "Good night."

He gathered her closer and she could feel him tugging gently at her unbound hair. "What are you doing?" she asked.

He chuckled sheepishly. "Spreading your hair over us. It's been one of my fantasies for days now."

She laughed. "Good grief. Just how many fantasies have you had, buddy?"

He kissed the back of her neck, and a sexual thrill shivered down her spine. "You have no idea, honey."

Kristin woke in the morning alone, and felt vaguely disappointed, even though she knew Derek was an early riser. Slipping out of bed, she padded into the shower, noting as she went the little twinges that reminded her of the night past.

He had awakened her in the wee hours by simply stroking his big hands up and down her torso, teasing her breasts into aching awareness and eventually moving lower. He'd slid his finger into her and rubbed gently until she'd exploded in his arms, then he'd taken her yet again before they'd drifted back to sleep for a little longer.

As she dried off, she studied herself in the mirror. Anyone looking at her would know something had changed, she thought ruefully. She was…glowing. And the person responsible for it had already put on the coffee downstairs, if the smell was any indicator.

Hurriedly, she dressed and ran down the steps. Maybe there would come a day when she didn't want to be with him every minute she could, but she doubted it.

He was in the kitchen, absorbed in the sports page and she paused in the doorway for a moment, drinking in the sight of the man she loved. His dark hair stuck out at odd angles. She'd seen him sleep before, and she knew why his hair looked like that. He buried his head in the pillow or in his arms. It struck her, for about the ten millionth time, how very unusual their relationship was. She already knew him as well as a wife of some years, she thought tenderly.

"Good morning." She smiled as she started across

the kitchen, intending to press her body to his and offer him a kiss.

"'Morning." Derek sent an abstracted smile in her direction but he didn't meet her eyes. Before she reached him, he turned away and picked up a new section of the newspaper, opening it and refolding it noisily to the page he wanted.

Her smile faded and she automatically detoured to the coffeepot on the counter to his left. The first moment of puzzlement began to give way to hurt as she poured herself a cup of coffee and carried it to the table. He still didn't look up, didn't speak again, and her impatience grew in direct proportion to the hurt that made her chin quiver despite her best efforts to still it.

"Okay," she finally said, setting her coffee cup down with a snap. "What's going on?"

"Huh?" Derek glanced at her over the top of the paper.

"Don't pretend you don't know what I mean. You're doing your level best to ignore me this morning. I thought—I expected—oh, never mind!" She slapped a hand on the table and rose, uncaring that her coffee sloshed across the paper he'd laid there.

"Kris, honey, wait." He moved faster than she imagined he could, grabbing her arm before she could leave the kitchen. "I'm sorry," he said. "I'm just not used to sharing my morning yet." He wrapped his arms around her and she let him hold her, burrowing into his embrace and laying her head on his chest.

"You looked like you were a million miles away."

"I was…thinking."

"About what?" The steady beat of his heart reassured her, as did the warmth of his arms around her and the slow glide of his palms up and down her back.

His hands stilled. "Deb," he said quietly. "I was thinking about Deb."

Kristin said, "Oh," in a small voice and fell silent. He expected questions but when she didn't say anything else, he relaxed and let himself savor the feel of her in his arms.

The moment she walked into the kitchen, he'd realized his error. Deb had hated his habit of rising early and slipping out of bed to read the paper, although she'd never said so flat out. She'd just been snippy and cool when she came down later, and he'd usually beaten a hasty retreat since he'd assumed that her first-thing-in-the-morning bad mood just needed time to mellow into her more usual placid temperament.

It wasn't until they'd gone to counseling a year later that he'd found out how it bugged her, that her bad mood was a result of his behavior. He'd been happy to change and it hadn't taken much. She didn't want to get up with him. All she'd wanted was a little nudge and a good morning kiss before he got up and left her dozing.

How could he have forgotten that? He'd felt guilty as hell so he'd immediately buried his head in the paper, hoping the moment would pass. Tomorrow morning, he'd make the effort for Kris.

She was quiet in his arms, and he savored the feel of her soft curves, marveling at his good fortune. How had he gotten lucky enough to find this kind of physical compatibility with one of his best friends? Slowly, he ran his hands down her back to her hips, tugging her more firmly against him and leisurely rubbing his hips against her, feeling the insistent rise of desire shorten his breath as his flesh firmed and filled.

He dropped his head and sought out the soft hollow just beneath her ear, nuzzling into the warm space, then tugging on her earlobe with light nips. Kristin shuddered, lifting her face to his and without hesitation, he took her mouth even as he reached down and put his hand beneath one of her thighs. She willingly lifted her leg and twined it around his hips while balancing on the one remaining, opening herself to allow him to boldly press himself against the warmth of her opened thighs.

He shoved his tongue into her mouth, suddenly feeling a burning need to brand her. She was going to be his wife. His wife! He hadn't allowed himself to think about marriage again after Deb—no. He wasn't going to go there. When he kissed her with renewed passion, she kissed him back with abandon, but when he reached beneath the little denim skirt she wore, she said, "Wait. Derek, we can't! Mollie—"

"Never wakes up much before nine," he reminded

her. "It's barely seven. But if it makes you feel better..." He lifted her with his hands beneath her bottom, and as she circled his hips with both legs and locked her arms around his neck, he carried her across the kitchen to the bathroom in the front hallway. Once inside, he closed the door firmly, then turned and leaned Kristin's weight against it. It was dark and cozy and though he could have turned on the light, he found he liked the clandestine feeling. He fumbled to pull the little skirt out of his way— and froze when he realized she wore no panties beneath it.

"Just what do you think you're up to?" he said, laughing and trying to sound stern at the same time.

She laughed, too, lifting her face for his kiss again. "I don't believe I'm the one who matches that description."

His amusement faded as he fondled the warm, smooth globes of her buttocks, exploring the tender flesh in her hidden folds. He made a rough sound of delight when his seeking fingers encountered slippery heat, and slowly, he let her slide down to stand on her own feet. He probed deeper with one finger before withdrawing, spreading the sweet moisture over her, delving again and again to repeat the process until she was twisting and crying against him.

He wanted her in every way there was, and though his own body was rigid and aching with the need to be inside her, there was something more he wanted to do, something he'd been fantasizing about in hot, erotic dreams for the past week. Slowly, he lowered himself to his knees and she clutched at his shoulders. "Derek, what…?"

"Hush," he said. "Let me taste you."

"Oh, no," she moaned. She covered her feminine mound with one hand but he only kissed and nibbled around the edges of her palm until she relaxed. Then he drew her hand away, returning it to his shoulders so that both of his were free to press against her inner thighs and widen her stance. He buried his nose in the sweet, spicy curls and inhaled deeply. "Ah, Kris, you're beautiful."

He'd said it before and he knew it was inadequate, but it was all his feeble brain could come up with at the moment. Slowly, taking his time, he licked a line along the curl-covered folds of tender flesh, tasting the dew he'd drawn forth. As her body gave way beneath his probing advances, he curled his tongue and thrust deep inside her, then found the tiny button of her desire and flicked it back and forth relentlessly, gauging her response in the shifting motions of her hips and the small cries she made above his head.

He was so hard he ached, and he finally pulled away long enough to rise and shove down the baggy pajama bottoms he wore and free himself. Kristin sagged against the door, but he slid his hand down her arm to capture her palm and drag it to him.

"Touch me," he said in a hoarse whisper, folding her fingers around his rigid length. Her hand was small and warm and he almost whimpered aloud at the exquisite sensation as she tentatively began to explore him. He did groan aloud when she found the small bead of moisture that had already escaped his control and spread it all around the throbbing head, her tentative touch so thrilling that he felt like throwing his head back and howling out his pleasure.

"Show me what to do," she implored.

"Like this." He put his hand over hers and began a slow rhythm. He showed her how tightly to grip him, how fast to stroke, and within moments she proved so apt a pupil that he was thrusting his hips into her hand and gritting his teeth as the inescapable conclusion to such shattering pleasure rose higher and higher. "Wait," he finally choked out.

He pulled her hand away with frantic haste and reached for her in the darkness, clasping her by the hips and yanking her up and onto him in a single wild motion. Immediately, he leaned forward, pinning her against the door. He'd prepared her so well that she came almost immediately as he thrust deep into her, driving her relentlessly up and over the edge so that she was arching and crying in his arms as her body rippled with contractions around him. He couldn't wait, couldn't last, and he let the dance of passion whirl him into his own release as he came heavily into her, his weight shoving her so hard against the door he knew he probably would bruise her. But his body didn't belong to him, didn't want to obey his commands. He could only cling to Kris and bury his face in her neck as he poured himself into her receptive body, her arms and legs anchoring him to the sweet reality of his new world.

He was gasping for air when the world finally

stopped spinning. Slowly he straightened. Kris's legs slid limply down to the floor but he didn't let her go because she felt as floppy as a rag doll to him.

"Hey." He had to stop, clear his throat and start over. "Are you okay?" He could actually feel himself blushing. God, no wonder. He'd acted like a man marooned on an island for years without sex.

"I'm fine." Her voice was dreamy and soft, and amazingly, he felt a twinge of renewed desire stir him. It was the first time in his life he really understood the phrase "ruled by his hormones." *His* hormones were very definitely in control. And what they wanted was sex. With Kris. Anytime, all the time.

Slowly, he lifted her away from him and set her down. He snapped on the lights and cleaned himself up in a few quick motions, then turned and gathered a folded pad of toilet tissue. When he dropped to his knees in front of her, she uttered a startled squeak.

"Wha—?" She tried to close her legs when she realized what he was doing, but he held her thighs apart with gentle, yet inexorable fingers and gently blotted her sensitive flesh. Then, unable to resist, he leaned forward and pressed a kiss to the soft tangle of curls, letting his tongue lap at her just one time.

She nearly jumped out of her skin, and he chuckled as he rose to his feet. "We'll get back to that later," he told her in a deep, satisfied voice before letting her go.

Nine

He took her hand and started back to the kitchen, leading her across to the breakfast nook and drawing her onto his knee. He was supremely conscious of the fact that she wore nothing beneath her skirt.

"So how did you lose your underwear?" he asked, smiling.

She shrugged, and a pretty pink lit her cheeks. "I guess I just forgot it this morning."

He laughed aloud. "Well, you can forget any morning. I promise not to complain."

She smiled. Then she laid her head on his shoulder. "We need to talk about birth control."

Birth control. Holy unplanned pregnancy. It was several seconds before he realized he'd spoken aloud. "I never gave it a thought," he said ruefully. "Deb never…she had trouble conceiving so we never… Is it the right time?''

''Probably not.'' Kristin raised her head and her gaze was steady and clear. ''I know you said you'd like more children, but I'd rather take our time and be sure you feel all right with it.''

''I'm going to feel all right with it,'' he said. ''But I'd like to have you to myself for a year or so before we add anyone new to our family.''

''All right. I'll take care of it today.'' She laid her head back on his shoulder.

She'd take care of it…? ''You're going on the Pill?''

''I don't know. That would be my first choice, but I'll see what my doctor says.''

''Do you mind? Because if you really don't want to, I can—''

''No.'' She put her hand over his mouth. ''I kind of like things the way they are now, without having to stop and think.''

He chuckled. ''The Pill's probably a good idea. Thinking doesn't seem to be something I'm real good at anymore when you walk through the door.''

''Good.'' There was a wealth of satisfaction in her voice.

They sat in silence for a few minutes. He couldn't remember when he'd enjoyed his morning more. Sitting here, with Kris in his lap, in his house, was almost perfect.

The moment he thought it, he felt disloyal. His life with Deb had been perfect. Or close to it. She'd taken care of the house and helped him with the clinic. She'd been the perfect spouse for a busy young vet trying to establish a practice. Deb had never wanted to work outside the home, and had looked forward to being a full-time mother.

On the other hand, he and Kris were going to have some things to work out along those lines. "Are you still going to want to work?" he asked her now.

She sat up in his lap and her answer was slow in coming. "Yes, although I may not open a full-time practice like I've been planning. I want to be home with Mollie and any other children we have. Once the new employee for the sanctuary comes on board, I could go back to my old schedule, working part-time from home."

"You don't have to work at all," he told her. "I'd be happy to support you if you want to be a full-time mom with no work commitments."

"Oh, no, I have to work," she said. "I mean, I *want* to work. And that reminds me—should we establish a joint account for the household expenses? We could put matching funds into it on a weekly or monthly basis."

He wasn't sure he liked the sound of that. "We might as well just combine everything," he said. "If you feel the need, you can bank your entire salary and I'll take care of you."

"No," she said hastily. "I wouldn't feel right about that. Besides, vets don't exactly compete with human doctors on the salary scale. Wouldn't one income be a stretch for us?"

He laughed, thinking of just how far his extensive wealth would go without stretching in the least. He supposed he'd have to tell her about it one day; but that wasn't something he wanted to get into right now. "Trust me, we wouldn't have any problems making ends meet."

"Still," she said stubbornly, "I'd rather pay my portion of everything."

He sighed. "Kris, we're becoming a family. Families don't split things down the middle. They do things together."

She hesitated, and her heart-shaped face fell. "I know. It's just that I have some financial obligations to conclude first."

Financial obligations? He idly wound one white-blond curl around his finger as he considered her words. Then he recalled something she'd said—or nearly said—the other day. What had it been, exactly? She'd been talking about opening a full-time accounting practice.

It would be a nice leap in my income level, let me finally get out from under—

Under what?

It sounded very much as though she had debts to pay, although he knew that couldn't be the case. When she'd insisted on selling her family home after her father's death, he'd purchased it as close to the upper end of fair market value as he could without making her suspicious that he was doing it for her. He'd wanted her to have plenty of money for her education with some left over for a home of her own.

Although so far, she'd lived in a rented town house since graduating from college.

That was something he had been meaning to discuss with her when he had time. Instead of pouring her money into rent, she should be paying into a mortgage for which she would get home ownership in return. Not to mention the benefits at tax time.

"You know," he said, "that's something I've been wanting to discuss with you. Why have you been renting instead of buying? I shouldn't have to tell an accountant the benefits of a mortgage."

She shrugged. "I haven't really had the time or desire to house-hunt."

"Even so," he persisted, "you could at least have bought a town house like the one you're in. It—"

"Derek." Her voice was soft yet implacable. "Has it ever occurred to you that one has to have a down payment to buy any sort of home at all?"

"Well, sure," he said, "but you should have plenty of money from selling me this place."

She tried to rise but he held her on his lap. "I don't," she said. "After Daddy died I had some…things to take care of."

He was shocked and he let it show. "You mean you have *nothing* left from that entire sum? What the hell have you been spending money on?"

Her face froze and her expression warned him he might have gone too far. "Gigolos. Gambling. And oh, gee, did I forget to mention I have a serious addiction problem that requires a couple thousand dollars a day?"

"Dammit, Kris," he said, not appreciating the sarcasm, "what's the big secret? I know you too well to believe anything as ridiculous as any of that."

"You don't know me as well as you think," she shot back. "You have absolutely no idea what I've been dealing with since Daddy died."

"I lost someone I loved, too," he reminded her evenly, wondering what in the hell that had to do with her finances.

"Yeah," she said, "but your someone wasn't up to her neck in debt, was she?"

There was a stunned silence in the room. Kristin's face grew red and her eyes filled with tears. "Dammit," she said quietly. "I wasn't ever going to tell you that."

"Tell me, anyway," he said. He was furious with himself for not being more attentive to her problems after her father died. Dammit! Paul had trusted him enough to name him Kristin's guardian in the event of his death...and he'd let his mentor down. He fought not to turn the feelings roiling inside him on her, controlling his irritation with her secretiveness. What exactly had she been trying to prove, dealing with it on her own?

She sighed. "Daddy had to borrow a lot of money in the first couple years of the sanctuary to get it up and running the way he wanted. If he'd lived, I'm sure we would have gotten back onto solid ground, but..."

"But he died and left you holding the bag," he finished for her.

"It wasn't like that," she flared.

"How could I not have known this?" he wondered aloud. "I was your guardian, for God's sake."

"You were only my guardian for a couple of months," she reminded him. "And don't you remember? When I said I'd been handling our bills for several years, you and Deb agreed that I could continue to do so with the help of my attorney and our accountant? I managed," she added defensively. "And after I sold the house to you, I was able to get the debt down to a very manageable balance."

"It's not paid off yet, is it?" he asked grimly. He had a vivid memory of the banker who'd arranged the sale of the house nodding approvingly at the generous amount he had offered for the property. Damned old weasel. Why hadn't anyone told him how much money she really needed?

"Well, no," she said. "It's not. Not quite. I could do it in a year working full-time but now I'll just—"

"I'll pay it off," he said. He felt a little sick to his stomach at the thought of Kristin laboring under what had obviously been a sizable debt for her entire adult life.

"You will not!"

"Yes," he said. "I will. You're going to be my wife, that means you're my responsibility."

Her face was red again but this time there was no trace of tears. "The last thing I intend to be is any man's 'responsibility,'" she said, making the word sound like an epithet. "I'll take care of my own problems."

He measured the determination written in her face for a long, tense moment. She glared at him, her green eyes spitting fire. Finally, he mentally crossed his fingers behind his back. "All right," he said, "you can handle your money problems by yourself." And the first thing Monday morning, he was going down to the bank and pay off the rest of what she owed. The bank could just tell her they'd made a mistake, or that some other creditor had paid what they owed her father. It wasn't as if he'd ever miss such a small amount.

They began packing her things Monday evening. Derek had just taken a load of winter clothes over to his house while Kristin tossed the contents of her drawers into a big trunk she'd had since college.

Her flying fingers paused on the T-shirt she was folding and she sank onto the edge of her bed, hands dropping into her lap. She couldn't believe how quickly everything was falling into place. Just as he'd said, Derek had begun the process of acquiring a marriage license earlier in the day, and they'd made appointments for their blood tests.

It was hard to imagine that only five short weeks ago he'd been telling her that a marriage between them was a ridiculous notion.

The rest of the weekend had been heavenly. They'd spent the day together with Mollie on Sunday, and that evening, he'd driven her over to her town house to pick up clothing for work on Monday. She'd asked if he was sure he wanted her to move in so quickly, and he'd only smiled. "Mollie and I want you with us," he'd said, "the sooner, the better."

Wistfully, she thought that the ideal response would have been a declaration of love, but she knew that while Derek cared about her, he didn't love her. He thought of her as a capable housekeeper, a great baby-sitter and a trusted friend. And as a lover, now. He wanted her, of that she was sure, but he wasn't about to let his desire for her mesh with any more intimate feelings.

The telephone rang and she rose automatically. She needed to call tomorrow to have the service stopped, she remembered as she lifted the handset. "Hello?"

"Hello, Kristin. It's Rusty. Is it true?"

"Is what true?" She tucked the phone between her ear and shoulder as she returned to her folding and packing.

"A little bird told me you and Derek are getting married."

"Goodness!" She was truly startled. "There are no secrets in this town, are there?"

"Oh, you'd be surprised." His voice was amused. "Your news, however, has gotten around. I would say congratulations but I'm too busy kicking myself for not talking you into dating me first."

She laughed. "Sorry."

"You two sure managed to keep things quiet," he continued. "Even at Summerfest, no one had any idea you were more than friends."

She was beginning to feel uncomfortable. "I'm kind of tied up here, Rusty. Was there something you needed?"

"As a matter of fact, there is." His tone changed, became more confidential. "I've been thinking about the money that's missing. Have you pursued it any further?"

"I haven't had much time since Friday," she said, "but nothing's leaped out at me. Whatever was done was hidden very carefully."

"I'm really concerned about the sanctuary's reputation as well as Cathie's," he said. "She's dead. She can't defend herself. I spoke to one of the bank officers at the Rotary Club meeting today and he alluded to her being in debt. I couldn't pry without making him suspicious, but I'm afraid our fears may be well founded. I think Cathie probably took the money to alleviate some personal problems she was having."

"Oh, no. I was so hoping…"

"I know. So was I," he said. "But there's no help for it now, and even if we do go public I doubt we have a hope in hell of getting the money back."

She sighed heavily, her heart aching. "You're probably right."

"So I think we should just write it off as a learning experience," he continued. "I won't tell anyone else what happened and if you don't either, we can protect Cathie's memory. I'll tell the board that you feel our current financial system needs more checks and balances, and establish a more stringent way to release funds so no one can ever do this again.''

She felt like an ant in the path of a steamroller. ''Maybe that would be best,'' she said cautiously. ''But what if it wasn't Cathie?''

''If it wasn't, and they try it again, we'll catch them,'' Rusty said confidently. ''If it was her, it won't occur again and we'll know, right?''

She nodded, then realized he couldn't see her. ''I guess so. All right.''

''Okay,'' said Rusty. ''If this works, we may not even have to alert whoever takes the job eventually that there was a problem.''

She woke in the middle of the night and immediately her mind turned to the problem of who had embezzled the money from the sanctuary. She lay on her side in Derek's bed, with his big body spooned around her and his hard arm circling her and she stared into the darkness as her mind raced.

''What's wrong?'' Derek's voice from behind her was little more than a quiet whisper but her body jolted in surprise.

''I was just thinking,'' she said. ''I didn't wake you, did I?''

He yawned. ''I'm not sure what woke me. But I could tell you weren't asleep. What's the matter?''

''I had lunch with Rusty last week and he seems certain Cathie was the embezzler,'' she said. She told him about her lunch with Rusty on Friday and then his telephone call earlier. ''But…''

"You don't think Cathie did it?"

"No. That's bothered me from the minute I found the discrepancies. One of the reasons I've been having such trouble imagining Cathie stealing from the sanctuary was because of her love for the project. Daddy chose her because she shared his vision."

"And she didn't need the money, anyway," he said.

"What do you mean?"

"Cathie came from a wealthy family," Derek said. "She had a trust from her grandmother that kept her in comfort. Didn't you ever wonder why she never asked for a raise? In fact, one year while you were in college, the board tried to give her a raise and she refused."

"I didn't know that. Why didn't you tell me when I first mentioned my concern that she might be embezzling?"

"Because I doubted it was true and it wasn't my place to share information she'd told me in confidence. She didn't want people to know," Derek said. "I can understand why. When people find out someone's wealthy, their perceptions of that person change."

"I suppose," she said slowly, wondering at the vehemence she heard in his tone, "that could be true." Then she forgot all about what they'd been saying as a new possibility occurred to her. "Derek! What if Rusty is the one who took the money?"

"Rusty? Why would he?"

"I don't know," she said. "He has awfully expensive tastes. Do you think his business does well enough to support two foreign cars, a country club membership, a Rolex and designer suits?''

Derek considered for a moment. "I don't know," he said at last. "No one I ever knew got rich selling insurance. It's a decent living but…''

"And his family was local," she added. "Not wealthy at all. Quite the opposite, in fact.''

She felt Derek shrug from where he still lay behind her. "It's possible," he said.

"It would explain why he doesn't want to contact the police," she said. "That's the first thing I would have done if he hadn't discouraged it.''

"Maybe you'd better do it first thing tomorrow," he suggested. "Without Rusty.''

"Maybe he intended to replace the missing money. I bet he never intended for anyone to know about it, but when Cathie was killed and I found it, he blamed her.''

"Whoa," he said. "That's a lot to assume without any proof.''

"Yes, but it's possible, right?''

"It makes sense," he said slowly, and he sounded a lot more awake. "He's the person other than Cathie who knew the most about the sanctuary's finances. And serving as the treasurer, he might have had the opportunity to cook up a false account or two.''

"That's what I'm going to start looking for first thing in the morning," she said. "So far, all I've done was check and recheck figures to be sure they all match. Now I guess I'll start looking for anything fishy.''

They lay silently for a moment, then Derek spoke again. ''Do you think there's a possibility that she and Rusty were involved in it together?''

''Not a chance,'' she said immediately. ''Cathie couldn't stand Rusty. She always said his ego was bigger than the Goodyear blimp.'' Then a horrible thought occurred. ''Do you think…could he have arranged her accident somehow?''

Derek's arm tightened around her waist. ''I don't know the answer to that. But now you've really convinced me that you need to get law enforcement involved tomorrow.''

She sighed. ''God, this just gets worse and worse, doesn't it?''

''Yeah,'' he said. ''It seems that way.''

She glanced at the clock. ''One-thirty-seven. I can't call anyone for a few hours yet.''

Derek pulled her closer, stroking his palm along the curve of her hip in a comforting gesture. She savored it for a moment, and eventually her disturbing thoughts receded as she felt him stirring and growing. Her bottom was nestled into the curve of his body and she squirmed against him, rubbing back and forth over his rising flesh. His hand crept up to cup one breast and he gently rotated his palm over her nipple. ''You know, it's a real shame that we're both awake in the middle of the night.''

She laughed breathlessly as her body grew warm

and lethargic. "Yeah, I wonder what we could do that would help us get back to sleep."

"We'll have to think of something." Derek's hand slipped down her body and slid between her legs. He lifted her leg over his thigh, then trailed his fingers along the widened V he'd made. She gave a broken cry of pleasure as he brushed over the sensitive feminine folds, touching her there with deft, careful strokes that gently aroused her. His fingers were quickly bathed in moisture and as he slid one deep inside her, she moaned and reached back to pull him hard against her. "What are you doing?"

"Having fun." His voice was rough and deep.

"I want you—inside me," she panted. "Please?"

"In a minute." His clever fingers wove tiny patterns over her trembling flesh, seeking out the pleasure point that seemed to be drawing her whole body into a taut, needy knot. "I want you to come for me first."

"Derek—" But she never completed the thought. A startling wave of sensation burst through her and she cried out, shuddering and arching in his arms. She was dimly aware of him touching her again and again, and yet again, as she was hurled into the maelstrom of her own climax.

Her body hadn't fully quieted when she felt Derek withdraw his hand and roll her onto her stomach. He slid an arm beneath her and pulled her up onto her knees and in the same moment, slid the hard column of his erection into her, pushing his hips hard against her buttocks. The position angled her up for a shockingly deep penetration and she buried her face in the pillow as she screamed.

"Am I hurting you?" He stilled at once.

"No," she said. "Oh, no!" She rocked forward and back. "Just move!"

"Oh, yeah." There was strain in his voice and she felt his muscles bunch and flex. He braced one hand on the bed beside her as he began to slide in and out of her, thrusting with steady, strong strokes. He pulled almost completely out, then lunged forward and embedded himself deeply.

She was crying out with every thrust, another level of sweet tension building and building, and this time when she came she felt the repeated pulses of his release jetting deep inside her, flooding her with the proof of his desire. As his taut muscles gave way, Derek slowly collapsed on her, his weight pressing her into the bed. He kissed the back of her neck, then rolled slowly aside and gathered her into his arms again.

"Why the hell did I ever think marrying you would be a bad idea?" he said above her head. "I've slept better since you moved in than I have since Deb died."

His arms were possessive, his tone tender, but Kristin's heart shriveled at his words. It wasn't that she begrudged Deb's place in his life. Or his heart. It was only that she wanted there to be a little space for *her,* as well. But it seemed to her that no matter what she did, it only served to remind him of his loss.

A vivid memory of their discussion of wedding plans played in her head. She *had* always envisioned a chapel and a lavish white dress with all their friends around them, but it had been obvious that Derek dreaded the notion. She'd seen Deb's and his wedding album. They'd had exactly that type of traditional affair. So she would do whatever he wanted if it would help him not to be reminded of what he'd lost. A big white wedding would have been fun and special, but she wanted him more than she wanted any silly ceremony. And even though she knew he didn't love her, she could hope that maybe someday when his heart healed…someday…

She woke when he did in the morning and instead of going downstairs and making coffee, Derek was almost late for work when she joined him in the shower. She slipped in behind him and circled his waist with her hands, pressing her long, lean curves against him from the back while her hands slipped down to stroke and cup the male flesh at his groin.

He let her take the lead as long as he could, let her fondle and rub and squeeze, but his self-control, always tenuous in the morning, eroded quickly. Spinning around, he bent her over the bench at the back wall of the shower, widening her stance by simply pressing himself between her spread legs. She was beautiful from this angle as well, the twin globes of her bottom glistening with beads of water. He tossed the loose mass of her hair over her shoulder, then positioned himself and slowly pushed into her, enjoying the sight of her soft pink flesh welcoming him, loving the feel of her body accepting every inch of him until his hips were solidly cradling her buttocks and he was buried to the hilt. She was warm and wet and making little sounds of pleasure and he marveled yet again at how he could have not realized what he would be missing without her in his life.

He was happier than he'd been since he'd first learned Deb was sick. Happier, maybe. The thought made him flinch, but he knew it was true. Deb had always welcomed his lovemaking but she'd never seemed to catch fire in his arms the way Kris did, or heaven forbid, initiated passionate moments. She'd never followed him into the shower, though she'd gone willingly enough when he'd indicated that was what he wanted.

Deb would have done anything to please him, but he wasn't certain he'd ever really been able to show her how much pleasure her own body was capable of. With Kris...he looked down at himself as he thrust in and out of her, then reached one hand around to search through her nest of curls until he found the sweet little button he sought. He pressed and circled and almost immediately, she gave a strangled cry and began to convulse around him.

He smiled, teeth gritted as he fought off his own finish, but her pleasure was too much to resist, and he began stroking in and out faster, harder, deeper, giving himself completely to her. His climax shivered down his spine and caught fire deep in his groin, surging up and exploding in heavy, pulsing waves of release as her body milked his length and coaxed the last drops of desire from him.

"Good morning," he gasped as he slipped out of her.

She turned to him, face radiant, and his heart skipped a beat as he drew her into his arms. God, she was beautiful. And her eyes… "Kris," he said before he even knew he was going to speak, "you love me, don't you?"

Her eyes widened and he felt her body tense for a second before she relaxed again. Her gaze softened as she searched his. "Yes," she said. "I love you, Derek."

He couldn't hide his relief as he bent to kiss her, and his heart swelled with satisfaction. "Good," he said. "I was hoping I hadn't read you wrong." He kissed her, lingering over it. "I need you, Kris," he said, clearing his throat. "I never thought I'd want another woman in my life, but now I can't imagine it without you."

He knew he wasn't imagining the pleasure that lit her face at his words as they finished showering and started their day.

Ten

Derek took Mollie to day care after breakfast on his way to the clinic.

"See you at dinner," he said to Kristin. "What are you going to do today?"

"I want to work this morning," she said, "and then I'll go over to the town house and try to finish packing."

"All right." He kissed her. "I'll see you at supper, I guess. Tonight I'll help you unpack."

She nodded. "Hope your day goes well." She stretched on tiptoe to kiss him, then bent to cuddle Mollie. She still felt like she was living a dream and she smiled as she waved them off and headed into the kitchen to pour herself a cup of coffee before starting to work.

Then she had a thought. It was eight-thirty now. In a short while, Rusty would be in his office, if he wasn't already. She reviewed her thoughts from the night before and a grim fury settled over her. If she was wrong, she would apologize until the cows came home. But she wasn't. She knew it.

There was a stack of mail that Derek apparently had opened and not dealt with on the counter a short distance from the coffeepot and she picked it up. It would be safer and out of the way in his office, so she picked it up as she moved toward the hallway to get her purse and keys.

She took the envelopes in and laid them in the center of his desk but as she walked out again, her hip brushed the edge of the desk and a different pile of papers slid to the floor. Yikes. Clearly, Derek could use her skills with paperwork, she thought with amusement. She retrieved all the papers and began to stack them again, idly noting that they were bank statements.

Behind the letterhead that read Quartz Forge Bank of Pennsylvania, an unfamiliar logo caught her eye. Manhattan Trust. Manhattan Trust? Hmm. Weird. Why wouldn't he have all his money at the Quartz Forge bank? She noted the balance: twenty-seven million, four hundred twenty-eight thousand—

Whoa. That was a mistake. Someone had screwed up the placement of the decimal point in that figure. She'd better circle it and tell Derek to call his bank immediately…and then her brain ground to a halt.

She took a closer look at the statement. There were

transactions in the millions in several places. Withdrawals, to be exact. This account had held over thirty million at the beginning of the month. Twenty-seven million dollars. Oh, my God.

Her hands began to shake. She felt breathless, and she gasped repeatedly for air. Derek had twenty-seven million dollars lying around in a bank in New York City. Then she realized he probably had a lot more than that. She'd bet anything those sizable transactions were stock buys.

Oh, my God.

Where had he gotten— It didn't matter. He must have been wealthy when he came here. But why keep it a secret? Her cheeks burned as she remembered explaining about her father's financial miscalculations, and her subsequent plan to pay off the debt.

Why on earth hadn't he ever told her? Had Deb known? Then she realized what a stupid question that was. Deb had known him since they were in high school together. Of course Deb had known.

Which meant that he'd kept it secret from her, Kristin…and probably never had intended to tell her.

God, no wonder he'd told her that he'd pay the bills and she could keep her salary. He must have thought that was hilarious!

Her chest hurt and she realized she was holding her self-control together by the barest of threads. Forcing herself to take deep breaths, she carefully laid the statement back on top of the stack. Her hands were shaking so badly she was afraid to pick up her coffee cup so she left it where it was on the desk.

Then she turned and walked out of the room.

She'd have to pack everything she'd already unpacked. He'd lied to her. She couldn't live with a man who would deceive her like that.

A sob burst out of her. She clapped a hand over her mouth and sank down on the bottom steps of the stairway in the hall. All these years, she had believed she knew Derek so well. She'd clutched all the little details of his life to her and been so—so *smug* about how well she knew him.

And all the time she hadn't known him at all.

Why would a man who could live like a king reside in what was a nice, but certainly not an opulent home? Why would he work? Drive a rather average American-made car? Questions bombarded her. Was he generous with his money? Was he a philanthropist—?

The donation. Oh, God, the million-dollar donation the animal sanctuary had received not long after Derek had come to town. Her father had been so thrilled, though he'd wanted terribly to thank the donor, who had remained anonymous.

Anonymous, her fanny. Now she knew exactly who the unknown soul of generosity had been.

Hurt sliced through her, so sharp and deep that she actually made a small sound of pain. Why had he hidden this from her? Her thoughts whirled around and around, making little sense as the hurt grew and expanded within her. She'd thought everything she'd ever wanted was within her reach. She had the man she loved and his beautiful daughter. But he *wasn't*

the man she loved, was he? He was a stranger. One
she didn't understand at all, and one who apparently
liked it that way. One to whom she wasn't important
enough that he would consider sharing the real story
of his life.

Tears rolled down her cheeks. She'd known he
didn't love her. But she'd thought, given time and
the powerful sexual attraction they shared, that marriage and sharing all it entailed would bring him
around. She'd thought she could earn his love, she
saw, because she'd assumed she knew him well
enough to predict his behavior. Now…what?

What could she do now?

She rose and snatched a tissue from the powder
room in the hallway. Blowing her nose and blotting
her eyes, she took a deep, quavering breath. She'd
have to get her act together by the end of the day
when Derek came home because there was no way
she could repack and move all her stuff in one day.
That was the only thing she was sure of.

Then she remembered what she'd been about to
do. Rusty. That was one thing that couldn't wait. Because if she was right, she was going to have to get
the police involved.

But if she hurried, ran over there right now, she
could get it over with quickly, and then get back here
and pack. If she worked hard enough, she might be
able to get most of her things packed again before
Derek got home.

Another sob threatened and she hastily spun and

headed for the table where her keys lay. *Don't think about it. Focus on Rusty.*

She repeated the words like a mantra the entire way to Rusty's office, and was incredibly relieved to see one of his little European sports cars parked in its usual spot. If she'd had to wait—and think—she wasn't sure she could have kept herself from breaking into tears.

Jumping out of her car, she ran up the steps to the landing and entered the foyer of Rusty's insurance office.

She'd always loved the subdued blue, cream and soft green hues in which the reception area was decorated, but today she looked at it with fresh eyes. Both the pictures on the wall were original paintings by a well-known East coast artist. The patterned rug on the floor was closely woven and for the first time, she realized it was probably old and probably had cost a fortune, as had the graceful mahogany furniture that decorated the entire room. Everything matched. There were fresh flowers in a sparkling crystal vase on a side table. Baccarat?

"Kristin!"

Her reflections were interrupted by Rusty's voice and she jumped. "Hi, Rusty."

"I'm not open yet but you're always welcome. Would you like a cup of coffee?" He looked as perfectly groomed as he always did in an expensive summer suit with leather loafers and the Rolex she'd seen before.

Was it her imagination or did his eyes look anxious? "No, thanks. I just came to talk for a moment. I won't take up much of your time."

"All right." He indicated a small sofa. "Would you like to sit down?"

"Thank you." She took a deep breath as he seated himself in an adjacent wing chair. Where to begin? How did one go about accusing someone else of embezzlement and possibly murder? She cleared her throat nervously. "I, ah, I came to talk more about the missing money."

"Oh." Rusty lowered his voice, tugging at the end of his silk tie. "Have you found out something about it?"

"I think so." She sat back in her chair. "I believe you stole the money, Rusty. You're the only other logical choice."

A dull red flush climbed his cheeks. "That's ridiculous. Why would I—"

She waved a hand around the room. "Why, indeed? Appearances are nice but are they worth going to jail for? If I call the police and tell them everything I know and what I suspect, will your bank statements and your past income tax forms bear out all this luxury?" Then she leaned forward. "Did Cathie know?"

There was a tense silence.

"No." The word slipped out and Rusty sagged in the chair. He passed a hand over his face. "Although I think she suspected."

"Did you have anything to do with her death?"

"No! Of course not." He looked sincerely shocked. "What kind of man do you think I am?"

"I don't know," she said. A wave of sadness surged. "I don't seem to know the men around me nearly as well as I thought I did." She rose from the chair. "Do you want to get your coat and come with me?"

"Come where?" He blinked at the abrupt change of subject.

"To the police station," she said impatiently, starting for the door. "Where else? You embezzled money, Rusty."

"Dammit, Kristin!" Rusty's voice was frantic. He followed her out the hallway to the front door. "Look, this can be fixed. Just give me some time to pay back the money I borrowed."

"You didn't borrow it," she said sternly. "You stole it from a nonprofit organization doing charitable work. There's a big difference."

"Okay," he said, shrugging. "I stole it." He caught at her hand. "But—"

The door slammed open. "Get your hands up where I can see them!"

The noise and yelling voices were paralyzing and she froze as three uniformed men suddenly rushed into the room with guns drawn. Guns! Slowly, she raised her hands in the air, but the officers rushed right by her and slammed Rusty against a wall. As she gaped in astonishment, he was searched and cuffed and read his rights.

"Kris." A deep, quiet male voice, a familiar voice,

called her name and she turned back to the doorway as a fourth officer stepped aside and allowed Derek to enter the room. He crossed to her and took her elbows. "Are you okay?"

"Of course I'm okay." She pulled free and indicated the police who were escorting Rusty from the room. "What are they doing?"

His eyebrows rose. "They're taking Rusty into custody for suspected embezzlement."

"But…how would they know that? Are they sure enough to be arresting him?"

"You mean other than the fact that we all heard you elicit his confession?"

"Other than that," she said tightly.

"I called Walker Glave this morning and told him our suspicions," Derek said, mentioning the president of the board. "Apparently, Cathie had come to him the day before she died with information about it and he was waiting, trying to decide what to do. You were on his list of people to speak to about it, but when we talked, he decided to go to the police immediately."

"So the timing of the arrest was coincidental?" That was hard to believe.

"No," he said patiently. "When I realized where you were, I called them right away."

"How did you know I was going to talk with Rusty?" she asked.

Derek smiled. "Kris, I know you. When something's bothering you, you tackle it head-on. I was halfway to work when it dawned on me that the minute I left you alone you'd confront Rusty. And when I realized that, my blood ran cold. Anyone who is capable of embezzling that much money and blaming it on a dead woman who can't defend herself might be capable of a lot worse.''

"He said he didn't have anything to do with Cathie's death, that it was an accident."

"I bet he also said he didn't take the money."

She didn't smile. She couldn't. The phrase "I know you," brought her feelings of betrayal rushing back full force. When he moved to take her in his arms, she stepped back a pace without really thinking about it. "When were you going to tell me about your bank balance?" she asked. "I thought I knew you, too, but it turns out I was wrong."

His face changed, and her last hope that perhaps it was a mistake and he hadn't really deceived her died. His gaze flicked sideways at the cop standing nearby. "Could you excuse us for a few minutes, please?"

"Sure," the officer said. "But don't leave yet. The detectives are going to want to hear what you know about this guy." He hooked a thumb over his shoulder to where Rusty sat in the squad car in handcuffs.

Derek indicated a small room just beyond the office, an employee lounge where Kristin had come before for short meetings on sanctuary business. She hesitated a moment. The last thing she wanted to do was go into that little room with him.

Derek must have read her refusal in her face.

"Kris," he said in an implacable tone. "In here. Now."

Her temper flared and she welcomed it. Anything was better than the dull hurt that gnawed at her insides. "I don't want to talk to you." It felt childish but she was too close to tears to think of something more sophisticated to say.

"You don't have to talk. All you have to do is listen." Derek took her arm in an unbreakable grip. He wasn't hurting her but he didn't release her until he had towed her into the small room off Rusty's office and shut the door. "Now," he said. "Get it off your chest. You're mad because you think I hid my wealth from you on purpose."

"You did," she said. "All these years…" She shook her head. "I can't marry you now."

"What?" If she'd set a match to a dynamite stick, she couldn't have gotten much more of a reaction. It wasn't a shout, it wasn't a demand. It was a roar. "Why the hell not?"

"Because," she said. "I'd feel funny marrying a man for his money."

"I didn't think you would," he said. "I thought you were marrying me because you love me."

She flinched, and didn't speak. What response could she make to that?

"Kris." Derek dropped his voice to a low, intimate register. "Honey, will you give me a chance to explain? All you have to do is listen. Then, I promise, if you want to leave you can."

She couldn't look at him. It hurt too much. She

was incredibly humiliated that she'd been so wrong all these years about him. She thought she knew him. Ha! He was a multimillionaire.

"I grew up in a regular middle-class family just like you," he said. "My mom was a teacher, my dad was an electrician who owned his own company. When I was a junior in high school, they celebrated their twenty-fifth wedding anniversary by taking a trip to the Caribbean. They never came home."

"What happened?" There was remembered anguish in his tone and she wasn't hard-hearted enough to resist that.

"They were snorkeling when a boat came roaring around a rocky outcropping and plowed right into them. They were side by side and they both died instantly." He took a deep breath. "The young man who killed them was a Saudi playboy, a prince in line for his father's sheikdom."

Her eyes widened. She supposed she'd thought he was going to say something about insurance money.

"The sheik was furious with his son, but he still managed to avoid having that damned killer face prosecution."

She drew in a sharp breath. "But that's wrong!"

"Yeah." His laugh was slightly bitter. "The sheik gave my brother and me each ten million dollars— like that's supposed to make me feel better that Mollie will never know how terrific her grandparents were. He also kicked his son out of line to inherit, which was personally a lot more satisfying to me than getting any money." He drew a breath. "Anyway, my brother's a Wall Street whiz and he manages the money for me. I honestly don't think much about the fact that I'm…''

"Rich?"

"Well, yeah." He tried a tentative smile.

"You were the anonymous donor to the sanctuary."

"Guilty."

She felt the tears well. "You made my dad very happy."

"It made *me* happy," he said. "Your father had great vision. Without him, there would be no sanctuary. I just helped him realize his dream a little sooner than later."

There was a brief moment of silence.

"So," Derek said. "Are you ready to go home now? I'm sure we can talk to the police later."

"I guess," she said slowly.

"And the other?" A note of uncertainty entered his voice. "Will you stay?"

She couldn't prevent the involuntary, brief shake of her head.

"Why not?" he demanded. "I explained about the money. Kris, you know me better than I know myself in all the important ways. I should have told you before but I honestly didn't think about it. We love each other. How can you walk away from that?" There was a note of naked desperation in his voice now.

It was a moment before the sense of what he'd said jelled. "We…love each other?" she said faintly.

"Don't we?" Uncertainty shone in his eyes. "You told me you loved me."

"I do," she said softly, "but *you* never said you loved *me*."

He looked sheepish. "Of course I love you. It just took me a while to admit it to myself. I never would have asked you to marry me if I hadn't fallen in love with you." He paused. "Do you believe me?"

She shrugged. "You want a mother for Mollie. And companionship. And we share a lot of history. We've been friends for a long time."

"I've been friends with Faye for a long time, too, and I didn't ask her to marry me," he pointed out.

"A month ago you thought I was nuts for suggesting marriage. I know you want me now, but I'm not stupid enough to think that sex and love are the same thing."

"They are for this guy," he said, his eyes very blue and incredibly warm as he took her into his arms. "I love you, Kris. I didn't want to admit how empty my life was, but you dragged me out of my cave and loved me until I couldn't help loving you back. Please say you'll stay and marry me."

She smiled up at him as she wound her arms around his neck. "All right," she said. "I'll marry you."

"And love me forever."

"And love you forever."

And as he sought her mouth, she lifted her face to his, all doubt erased. Derek loved her. She'd waited patiently for him to grieve and begin to live again.

And all the while she'd quietly loved him, so quietly that she hadn't even realized it when he'd begun to love her in return. But now, now she knew.

And the future had never looked brighter.

*   *   *   *   *

Look for Anne Marie Winston's next book,
THE ENEMY'S DAUGHTER, part of
Silhouette Desire's in-line continuity
DYNASTIES: THE DANFORTHS,
in September 2004.

Silhouette® Desire®

**The captivating family saga of
the Danforths continues with**

Sin City Wedding
by
KATHERINE GARBERA
(Silhouette Desire #1567)

When ex-flame Larissa Nelson showed up on
Jacob Danforth's doorstep with a child she claimed was
his, the duty-bound billionaire demanded they marry. A
quickie wedding in Vegas joined Jacob and the shy librarian
in a marriage of convenience...but living as husband and
wife stirred passions that neither could deny—nor resist.

DYNASTIES: THE DANFORTHS

**A family of prominence...
tested by scandal, sustained by passion!**

Available March 2004 at your favorite retail outlet.

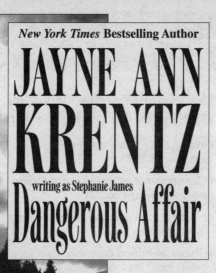

The Stolen Baby

Silhouette Desire's powerful miniseries features six
wealthy Texas bachelors—all members of the state's
most prestigious club—who set out to unravel the
mystery surrounding one tiny baby...and discover
true love in the process!

This newest installment continues with

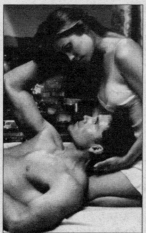

Pretending With the Playboy
by
CATHLEEN GALITZ
(Silhouette Desire #1569)

Meet Alexander Kent—
irredeemable playboy,
ladies' man and husband?
His undercover sting operation
required a wife, and prim
librarian Stephanie Firth
was perfect for the part...
until he started involving
his heart for real!

Available March 2004 at your favorite retail outlet.

DIXIE BROWNING

tantalizes readers with her latest romance from Silhouette Desire:

Driven to Distraction
(Silhouette Desire #1568)

You'll feel the heat when a beautiful columnist finds herself compelled by desire for a long-legged lawman. Can close proximity bring out their secret longings?

Available March 2004 at your favorite retail outlet.

COMING NEXT MONTH

#1567 SIN CITY WEDDING—Katherine Garbera
Dynasties: The Danforths
When ex-flame Larissa Nelson showed up on Jacob Danforth's doorstep with a child she claimed was his, the duty-bound billionaire demanded they marry. A quickie wedding in Vegas joined Jacob and the shy librarian in a marriage of convenience, but living as husband and wife stirred passions that neither could deny…nor resist.

#1568 DRIVEN TO DISTRACTION—Dixie Browning
An unofficial investigation led both Maggie Riley and Ben Hunter to sign up for a painting class. As artists, the advice columnist and ex-cop were complete failures, but as lovers they were *red-hot*. Soon the mystery they'd come to solve was taking a back seat to their unquenchable desires!

#1569 PRETENDING WITH THE PLAYBOY—Cathleen Galitz
Texas Cattleman's Club: The Stolen Baby
Outwardly charming, secretly cynical, Alexander Kent held no illusions about love. Then the former FBI agent was paired with prim and innocent Stephanie Firth on an undercover mission. Posing as a couple led to some heated moments. Too bad intense lovemaking wasn't enough to base forever on. Or was it?

#1570 PRIVATE INDISCRETIONS—Susan Crosby
Behind Closed Doors
Former bad boy Sam Remington returned to his hometown after fifteen years with only one thing in mind: Dana Sterling. The former golden girl turned U.S. Senator had been the stuff of fantasies for adolescent Sam…and still was. But when threats put Dana in danger, could Sam put his desires aside and save her?

#1571 A TEMPTING ENGAGEMENT—Bronwyn Jameson
He'd woken with a hangover—and a very naked nanny in his bed. Trouble was, single dad Mitch Goodwin couldn't remember what had happened the night before. And when Emily Warner left without a word, he *had* to lure her back. For his son's sake, of course. But keeping his hands off the innocently seductive Emily was harder than he imagined.…

#1572 LIKE A HURRICANE—Roxanne St. Claire
Developer Quinn McGrath could always recognize a hot property. And sassy Nicole Whitaker was definitely that. Discovering that Nicole was blockading his business deal didn't faze him. They were adversaries in business—but it was pleasuring the voluptuous beauty that Quinn couldn't stop thinking about.

SDCNM0204